HER SECRET

ASHOK BHASIN

HER SECRET

INDIA • SINGAPORE • MALAYSIA

Disclaimer

This is a work of fiction. All names, characters, and circumstances are the product of the author's fiction and any resemblance to real-life people or situations is purely coincidental.

PART - 1

Chapter - I

She opened the door of her car, sat down and said,

"Aerocity, Marriot."

The driver nodded and started driving.

Natasha had come to the office after 20 days. She lost her father after he suffered a cardiac arrest. Being the only child, she performed all rituals, which ended on the seventeenth day, but took two more days to come to her own. She lost her mother when she was 17. For the last 20 years, her father was both to her. That day, she went to her workplace, but she couldn't focus on work. At 3 pm, she got up and came out.

Natasha was the CFO of a company engaged in paint manufacturing. The Olympic Paints (India) Ltd., had an office at Gurugram, Haryana, the financial and technology hub near Delhi.

Soon, she was at J. W. Marriot, where Neelesh was waiting for her, sitting in the lobby on the left side after the entrance. He got up as he saw her entering. Both settled down. Neelesh said, "It was sad. It happened all of a sudden."

"Yes, it was unexpected. He was keeping good health," Natasha replied.

"I was there at the prayer meeting but couldn't talk much."

She kept silent.

"Still gloomy?" Neelesh asked.

"I feel as if I am left alone. It will take some time to come out of the situation."

"I can understand," Neelesh said.

Neelesh signalled to a waiter and asked for tea. Neelesh was a lawyer and met Natasha when he was handling an arbitration matter at her company. He said,

"People in huge numbers from the legal fraternity were there for your father's prayer meeting."

"You must know most of them?" Natasha asked.

"Some of them. They had all praises for your father. He was an upright, honest, knowledgeable and soft-spoken judge," Neelesh replied.

"Yes, I know," Natasha responded.

Just then, tea and some cookies were served. Neelesh poured it into the respective cups, put some sugar and handed one to Natasha.

"So, how was the day today at the office?" Neelesh probed further.

Natasha took a sip and said, "Colleagues keep coming for condolences. Not much office work got done."

"Archit must have dropped by?"

"Yes, he too came to my cabin and sat with me for about half an hour, consoling me. Archit is a nice man."

"Very few bosses behave like that. He is a thorough gentleman, always concerned about his employees."

"Yeah."

They both concentrated on having tea. Natasha's father, better known as Justice Chowdhary, had retired from the Punjab and Haryana High Court six months back. He had an apartment in Dwarka, but had to move to Chandigarh after he was elevated to the position of a Justice. Since Natasha's office was in Gurugram, she preferred her rented one-bedroom apartment near the office. She kept visiting Dwarka off and on. Her father also used to come from Chandigarh once a month.

Neelesh asked,

"You must be moving to the home in Dwarka now?"

"I am not sure, but for now, 'yes'. Today, I will go to my apartment in Gurugram. I have to pick up a few things. In a day or two, I will move to Dwarka."

"When your father had this attack, was he at Dwarka?"

"No, he was at my place. I immediately took him to Medanta Hospital. They took him into the intensive care unit, but soon, the doctors declared him dead."

"Shocking."

"Very shocking."

They finished the tea. Neelesh offered to drop her, but Natasha said she had a car waiting.

✦ ✦ ✦

While sitting in the car, Natasha was in a contemplating mood. Her father was a lawyer in Delhi and was later elevated to the position of Justice at the High Court in Chandigarh. When she was young, her mother scummed to blood cancer, perhaps in her final year in school. She studied accountancy for her graduation and was a qualified chartered accountant. Olympic Paints (India) Ltd. was her first job and she stayed on. Archit Mehra was the managing director. His wife was another director. The company had entered into a franchise with an American company. Two directors were Americans as per the contract terms, taking the number of directors at the company to four.

Natasha was appointed CFO about four years back and the management completely trusted her. She did her job diligently and honestly.

She was 37 years old a career-oriented woman and marriage was not her priority. She reached at her Gurugram residence. The next day was Saturday. She had decided to move to Dwarka home on Saturday. She got up and told the driver,

"Kishan, I need you to come tomorrow."

"Yes, madam," Kishan said.

Kishan was a new driver, referred by her old driver, Kuku, as a replacement. Kuku was visiting his hometown. Kuku was with her for the last seven years. She liked Kishan, too. He was well-mannered and disciplined. Drivers with these qualities were rare to find.

* * *

Neelesh had 15 years of standing in the bar. He got married when he was 27, but things started getting uncomfortable, and the marriage lasted for just a couple of years. His wife, Sujata, too was a lawyer. Finally, they decided to separate and filed a petition for mutual divorce. Initially, he had a good practice and earned a good reputation. During that period, he managed to buy a 3BHK apartment in Vasant Kunj. Now, the practice was on the decline thus, he converted one of the rooms into a home office.

He came in contact with Natasha when he had held a number of meetings with Archit and Natasha for an arbitration matter. Natasha was required to visit there during that period. They developed an affinity and started seeing each other regularly.

* * *

On Saturday, Natasha came to her father's home in Dwarka, she arranged for a part-time domestic helper who cleaned the house. Her Gurugram apartment, though small, was well furnished, and she had arranged the things as per her needs, a true bachelor pad. In contrast, the house in Dwarka was located in an old three-bedroom society apartment. Two bedrooms were well organized, the hall had old cane furniture. A lot of memories were attached to that house.

She moved around the house, entered her father's bedroom and opened the almirah. His clothes, mostly black trousers, white shirts and black coats, were there. There were a few polo shirts, which he used to wear when he was on vacation. The movement of a judge is usually restricted to his fraternity. She opened a safe box on the right side of the middle shelf. A few documents were lying there along with a few pieces of her mother's jewellery, perhaps as a memoir. Two of her father's savings account cheque books were lying there too. She closed the safe box. On the upper shelf were a few albums. She brought it out, sat on the bed and started going through them. It had pictures when she was young and used to go out with her mother and father. At that time, people took pictures on film roles and these were printed to be stored as a memory.

While she was glancing through these albums, she heard the doorbell. She got up and opened the door. It was Mehta aunty who lived on the same floor.

"*Namaste*, aunty," Natasha greeted.

"Natasha *beta*. I saw the lights were on and wondered if you were here," she said.

"Yes, aunty. I moved in today."

"That is good. You must live here."

"Yes, aunty."

"And if you need anything, you know where I stay. Don't hesitate," Mehta aunty said as she was leaving.

"Sure," Natasha responded before closing the door. "That was the way of life here," she thought. At Gurugram, neighbours won't bother you or check on you.

For the rest of the Saturday, she received two calls, one from Neelesh and another from Amar uncle, her father's old friend. She had a brief chat with them.

* * * * *

Chapter - II

It was a Sunday. The domestic helper had left after completing her chores. Natasha was checking her email on the laptop while sipping her coffee. She hadn't answered her emails in the last few days. She noted down the emails which needed immediate attention.

After lunch, she watched a movie on Netflix and took a nap. When she got up, she felt relaxed.

Around 6 pm, she opened the box, which was built in the bed in her father's room. Winter had started to set in, so, Natasha wanted a thicker quilt. With one hand, she held the lid of the box and with another she pulled out the quilt. At that time, she saw two black polybags under the quilt. She had not seen these before. She opened both bags inside the boxed bed. To her shock, there was money in it. She took out the bunch. Eagerly, she pulled out both the bags and closed the box. She brought both the bags to another room and ensured the front door was locked.

She took out all the cash and placed it on the bed. All the currency was in US dollars in denominations of 100. Ten bundles of $100 notes were bunched together by a rubber band, making it $100,000. There were 30 such bunches, making the sum $30,000,000.

Natasha stared in disbelief. She was shocked, angry, nervous and scared. She started trembling and could not believe her eyes. More than twenty crore rupees were in front of her eyes. She couldn't understand what to do. The first thing that came to her was to wrap up the currency and put it back in the bed.

She did that.

She caught two bottles of wine in her room, poured some into a glass and started sipping it. She was still not stable. Justice Chowdhary had the reputation of being an honest, upright and compassionate person. Everyone in the legal fraternity, lawyers, judges and close friends, were aware of his spotless reputation. Where did he get so much cash and that too in US dollars? Was it a bribe? She closed her eyes and leaned on the bed. She could never imagine her father accepting a bribe for a favourable judgement. She was sure but the more she kept thinking, the stronger her belief became that it was a bribe. When, who, where and how was it given to him? A series of questions started coming to her mind.

Justice Chowdhary's death was so sudden that even if he intended to confide in her daughter Natasha, he didn't get to tell her. Had she not opened the bed, she would have never discovered its existence. There could have been a possibility of not opening the bed, if not for years, for months.

She poured another drink and gulped it in one go.

Being well aware of the various taxation laws of the country, she understood she was in a tricky situation. She knew possessing foreign currency without legal documents was a serious offence under the Foreign Exchange Management Act, 1999 (FEMA). The burden to prove how she had so much foreign exchange was on her. Nobody was going to believe that she had recovered all of it from her father's bed, a person who was no more. She couldn't focus and figure out how to handle the situation.

However, Natasha was wondering how her father came in possession of so much foreign currency, particularly when his reputation throughout life was beyond any doubt.

Negative thoughts started taking over her mind. Was her father forcefully bribed? Was he blackmailed? What triggered the massive attack that resulted in his death? Was he under stress?

Amar Kant Joshi was a senior lawyer, and Natasha used to call him Amar uncle. Amar uncle and her father were friends from college. They used to share things. Amar Joshi's phone rang. He looked. It was Natasha.

"Hello, Uncle."

"Yes, *beta*, how is everything?"

"Uncle, can I talk to you for a minute?"

"Yes, yes, of course, *beta*."

"When had you last met father before his death?"

"A day before, why?"

"Nothing uncle, I was just wondering what triggered such a fatal attack. He was always so jovial."

"Yes. He was jovial and normal when I last met him," said Amar.

"Did he share any of the case decided by him?"

"No *beta*, a judge is not supposed to share such things."

"Yes uncle. It occurred to me that he might have discussed some matter, particularly after retirement," Natasha probed.

Amar thought momentarily and said, "No, nothing in particular. There was some casual talk about the last judgement he delivered, but I am sure he was not under stress."

"What was the judgement?"

"You seem to be quite upset. I assure you; your father was under no stress at all."

"Still, what was the judgement?"

"It was a PIL filed by an NGO restraining a builder from construction in the area marked as forest land. The builder was chopping trees somewhere on the Ridge towards Faridabad."

"Was it given in the favour of the NGO?"

"No, the judgement was in favour of the builder. The PIL of the NGO was dismissed on technical grounds."

"Technical grounds?"

"It means, the judgement was not given on merits. The PIL might have been filed quoting wrong provisions of law."

Natasha kept silent.

"Is there something that you come across or has anybody said something?" asked Amar uncle with concern.

"No, uncle. Not at all. It was only about the stress I thought of checking with you."

"Look Natasha, what has happened, has happened. I am sorry for your loss."

"Uncle, it is your loss, too."

"Definitely. I have lost my best friend. Why don't you come to our place? You will feel better when you talk to me or your aunty."

They disconnected.

* * *

Natasha opened her laptop and searched the High Court of Punjab and Haryana website. It had all the judgements listed in a year-wise manner. She scanned and came across the particular judgement, Amar uncle was referring to and started going through it. It was a seven-page judgement a short cryptic order. The builder was **M/s Cherry Hill Construction Pvt.** Ltd and the concerned project had six towers. About 40 percent of the construction was already completed. The NGO was writing letters to the concerned departments of the Haryana Government and observing that construction was continuing. Then the NGO filed the PIL that was dismissed. The bench had two judges. One of them was her father, Justice Chowdhary and another was Justice Mittal.

Natasha tried to recall Justice Mittal. His complete name was Arun Mittal. She had never heard of him. She noted the name of the lawyer representing the builder. It was one Vinod Goyal.

As she switched off her laptop, she wondered, "Could it be possible the builder bribed her father to get a favourable judgement?" No, she knew her father's track record was impeccable. But the cash lying in the boxed bed, was it telling a different story?

She was in no mood to prepare dinner. She took the bread and made some sandwiches. She poured one more drink and sat on the bed.

By the time she finished the drink and sandwiches, her mind was clear that she needed to get rid of money. But how? She would have to figure that out. It had to be done discreetly and she had to behave as if the money in the house was not in her knowledge.

* * *

On Monday, she messaged Archit Mehra, her boss, that she would prefer to work from home.

At about 11'O clock, there was a doorbell. She opened. It was Kuku, her former driver. Kuku was standing at the door with folded hands. He had tears in his eyes. He said, "Madam, I learned about *saheb* this morning. Kishan told me. It came as a shock. Saheb was so good to me. He was a father figure for me."

Natasha looked at Kuku. Her eyes, too were moistened. She consoled him and asked him to sit on the chair near the door. She said,

"When did you get back?"

"Today morning…"

"Kuku, let us bear this together. I know you must be very sad. It was in our destiny. Will you have a cup of tea?"

"No. Thank you, madam."

"Do you intend to start your job?"

"Yes, definitely, but I am worried about Kishan. He will become jobless."

"Kishan is a nice person. I will try to help him."

Natasha went inside and came out after about ten minutes. She said,

"Kuku, I talked to Neelesh, sir. He wanted a good driver. He needs one. You can ask Kishan to talk to Neelesh sir."

"Thank you, Madam."

"Do you have Neelesh sir's number?"

"Yes, madam," Kuku said. He got up, bowed a little and went out.

* * * * *

Chapter- III

In the evening, Natasha met Neelesh at the Marriot. They ordered a coffee.

"So, how was the day?" asked Neelesh.

"I decided to work from home," Natasha replied.

"Oh, you told me on the telephone. Still not stable?"

"No. It's ok, but the Dwarka house has a lot of memories. I kept looking at the pictures and other things."

Neelesh had a feeling that Natasha was looking sadder. He said, "Hey, I can understand your loss, but this is a part of life. This is bound to happen to everyone."

"Yeah, but it happened too soon."

"Yes, you have to control yourself. You are feeling lonely. You have to be strong. I am there with you, always."

"I know."

"By the way, thank you. The driver you recommended is good."

Natasha looked at him and thought whether she could rely on him and share the stash of cash she discovered at her father's house in Dwarka. She felt once the information was out of her mouth, it was out. She decided against it. Neelesh held her hand and started caressing it slowly. It felt good. She needed it. After some small talk, she asked,

"Neelesh, have you heard the name Vinod Goyal? He is a lawyer."

"No, is he practicing in Delhi?" Neelesh enquired. Natasha realized Vinod Goyal must be practicing in Chandigarh. She said,

"I don't know. Some colleague was asking about his reputation."

"Reputation?"

"I mean credentials. Whether he is reliable or not? It just occurred to me that perhaps you know him, being in the same profession."

"No. I have not heard about him, but I can find out if you want me to."

"Not really," Natasha said, placing her other hand on Neelesh's. It was reassuring.

"We should meet more often," said Neelesh.

Natasha smiled and said, "We do meet quite often."

"You shall not feel lonely," Neelesh insisted.

"Thank you for your concern."

Neelesh and Natasha kept chit-chatting for another half an hour before leaving.

* * *

M/s Olympic Paints (India) Pvt. Ltd. had an office at Golf Course Road, Gurugram. The company had a manufacturing plant in Alwar, Rajasthan. They were into manufacturing of paints, both domestic as well as industrial. The company had a turnover of about Rs 500 Crores.

Since the period the company had entered into a franchise with the US based-company, there were clear instructions that no bribe was to be offered for getting any job done to any government department, whether at a junior level or senior level. Archit, the MD of Olympic Paints and Natasha's boss, had agreed knowing that running a business in India was almost impossible unless you were willing to grease some palms. The rot in the system was deep and it was a necessary evil.

Natasha, the CFO was an asset for Archit. Whenever there was any roadblock in the business, he would discuss it with Natasha to know her views.

Sukhdev Singh, DGM had been in the company for the last twenty-three years. Natasha in turn used to rely upon Sukhdev. The message was long and clear to all the employees that no bribe should be given. The company followed and fulfilled all ethical and legal norms. The company had a good reputation in that context.

Still, if some matter involving underhand transactions came up, it would be discussed between Archit and Natasha. It was up to Natasha to manage it in a manner that the transaction was kept under wraps. She sometimes arranged the cash amount by raising false vouchers or paying it through consultants. They would inflate the consultant's fee to cover the bribe amount. For this purpose, the issue remained between Natasha and Sukhdev. Sukhdev would and had never discussed such issues with any of his colleagues in as much as he would not even admit such a transaction before Archit. That was how Archit got the work done and kept a clean record.

Natasha remembered that, before the American directors entered in the company, a couple of times, money was transferred abroad through Hawala operators. That job was handled by Sukhdev successfully. The company used to import chemicals at a lower value to save the customs duty. The differential amount between the actual purchase price and the invoice price needed to be remitted to the supplier sitting outside. Such differential amounts were transferred through Hawala operators, being unaccounted money. Such a practice of transfer is prevalent all over the world.

The Hawala system means money transfers hands without money movement officially. A person intending to transfer money would approach the Hawala operator in the country and hand over the money to the operator. The Hawala broker would call his counterpart in another country where the money will be transferred. The recipient sitting in another country gets the money. The Hawala operator would charge a nominal amount towards commission before handing over the money.

Natasha was sitting with Archit. They had an hour-long meeting to discuss some pending issues. The replies to emails received from vendors were to be sent. Natasha seemed to be in her usual form. After finishing the meeting, she returned to her cabin and called her secretary, Jasmine, to give her instructions on drafting the emails. Jasmine was more than just a secretary. She was efficient and knew how to address the letters to suppliers, buyers or government departments. She was just to be told once. Jasmine picked up her notebook and was about to go out when Natasha said,

"Will you please ask Sukhdev to come?"

"Sure, madam."

In another five minutes, Sukhdev entered Natasha's cabin,

"Good morning, madam,"

"Good morning," said Natasha and signalled him to sit down. She smiled and said, "So, how did work go while I was not in office?"

"As usual. A refund of Rs five crores from the VAT department is stuck. They are demanding money to release the refund."

"Who is looking into the matter?"

"Vinay Chauhan. He had brought it in the knowledge of Archit, sir."

"Then?" asked she.

"Archit sir, told him the refund is legally payable to the company. No money is to be paid."

Natasha smiled and said, "There is no illegality in the refund?"

"No, Madam, but the department can always cause delays."

"How long can they hold it?"

Sukhdev shrugged his shoulders and said, "Can't say?"

"Ok, we will figure it out. The company needs the funds. Why get it delayed?" Natasha replied.

"Shall I visit the VAT department?" Sukhdev asked.

"Wait. I'll tell you," Natasha said.

"Ok," said Sukhdev.

She remained silent for a couple of minutes and said, "Sukhdev, do you remember we had transferred some money to Hong Kong? I think it was a few years back."

"Yes, I remember."

"Who was the person?"

"Mulliani. I don't know the full name, but he is known as Mulliani."

"Is he still in business?"

"You mean the business of money transfer?"

"Yes."

"I have not met him for years. Is there some work?"

"Not immediately, but we may need his services. Can you find out whether he is still operating?"

"That's not difficult to find out."

Natasha smiled and said, "You may look into the VAT refund in a day or two. Please ask Vinay to keep the concerned person in the loop."

Sukhdev stood up, pushed the chair back and went out.

Natasha had decided to transfer the cash abroad but, she didn't know where and to whom. She was confident that transfer would not be and should not be inconvenient, as such transfers were quite common in the business circle. She had seen a number of advertisements from builders who used to claim that if one invested in property in Dubai, the person would be granted a resident visa and could open bank account in Dubai. She knew that in Dubai, even when large cash is deposited in the bank, no one raises an eyebrow. There was no income tax. Once she could deposit the money in her Dubai account things would settle down. She wanted to avoid keeping such a massive sum at home. She scanned through Facebook. There were DAMAC, EMMAR, Sobha and a lot more builders offering resident visas, Emirates card and opening of bank accounts. She came across a builder, Capri. Similar offers were there and the minimum price for a studio apartment was 500,000 Dirhams, equivalent to approximately Rs 10,000,000. Capri's representatives were at Delhi holding a workshop in the Westin Hotel in Gurugram. The ad also shared the contact numbers. There was nothing illegal in buying a house in Dubai or opening an account, even according to Indian laws, subject to legal transfer of money for buying an apartment.

She called the number and said,

"Capri?"

"Yes, please."

"My name is Natasha and I am interested in buying an apartment in your project."

"Madam, if it is convenient for you to visit, I'll explain everything."

"Where?" asked she.

"At Westin, Gurugram. We are here till 8 pm. My name is Mike Grage. You can contact me."

"Ok. I'll try to drop by."

"You are welcome, madam."

She came out of the office at about 6:30 pm. She got in the car and told Kuku, "We have to go to Westin."

"Ok Madam."

It took them 20 minutes to arrive at their destination. In the lobby itself, Capri had put up a stall. Natasha called Mike. Capri had taken a small seminar room on rent with eight tables with representatives attending to customers. Almost all tables were occupied, which meant people were interested in investing in Dubai. They waited for a table to become vacant. Five minutes later, she sat down with Mike, who explained the project.

The project had just launched and would take four years to complete. He explained the location, the materials to be used and so on. Natasha pretended to be listening but she waited for the crucial query. When Mike finished, she said,

"What is the minimum price for a studio apartment?"

"DHRM 500,000 and you see…." She didn't let him complete the sentence and said, "Ok, is that to be paid in one go?"

"No, you have to pay 20 percent of the price within 30 days of booking," Mike responded.

"And at the time of booking?"

"Five percent, you can pay now and balance 15 percent in next 30 days."

"What is all this about a resident visa and bank account?" Natasha enquired further.

"The UAE government is offering the resident visa for two years which can be renewed later. Once you get your resident visa, you have to apply for the Emirates card based on which an account can be opened in any bank in Dubai."

"Do I have to visit Dubai?"

"Yes, once and you may have to stay for five days. After that, our executives will be able to handle the Emirates card and the bank account process per your instructions. But to obtain a visa, you must be present in Dubai with your passport."

"All of this is legal?"

Mike smiled and said,

"Look at all the people here. It is all official and legal as per laws of both the countries."

Natasha kept quiet. Mike said eagerly,

"So, madam, which one would you like to book?"

"Are you camping here tomorrow too?"

"Yes, madam,"

"Right then, I'll confirm tomorrow," said Natasha and got up.

"Can I have your contact number?"

"Sure," Natasha told him her mobile number, which Mike noted in a diary.

At night, she got a call from Sukhdev that Mulliani was very much in business.

* * * *

Chapter - IV

Natasha and Archit had hour-long official meetings routinely to discuss the matters of the company. The next day while at the meeting, Natasha brought up the Rs five crore VAT refund issue. Archit said,

"Yeah, I know the concerned person in the government department is demanding money, something between two to three lakhs. Look at our country! The refund is legally entitled to us. The person is not doing a favour, still he is not ready to release the money unless he gets paid. These departments! You see, that is the reason foreign companies hesitate to come to India."

Natasha was listening. Archit said,

"Tell Vinay we will not pay anything."

"Sir, we should look at it from a business point of view. I am also not in favour of giving bribes," Natasha argued.

"What do you mean?"

"Sir, it is a refund of Rs. Five Crore and if it gets delayed, say for one year, the interest would work out between Rs 50-60 lakhs. What is the harm in paying Rs 2 lakhs? By paying the two lakhs, we can gain Rs 50 to 60 lakhs in interest. The proposition is not bad."

"Does the department not pay interest on delayed payment of refund?"

"Sir, one should consider himself lucky if he gets the principal amount."

Archit kept quiet, leaned back on his chair and said,

"You know how to convince your boss."

"Sir, I am simply talking about the company's interest."

"Ok, get it done. You know how to manage."

"Sure, sir."

They discussed the budgeting for the next financial year before closing the meeting.

* * *

In the evening, Natasha revisited Westin Gurgaon to close the deal with Mike. She paid the twenty percent, which was Rs. 2,000,000/-. Mike demanded a copy of her passport, recent photograph and the cheque. He filled in the particulars about Natasha Chowdhary on his laptop. It took about half an hour. Finally, he closed the laptop and said,

"It's done."

"How much time will it take to get the visa?"

"In 20 working days, you will get an entry permit. You will have to visit Dubai. Our staff will take care of all the other details. The passport will have to be submitted before the authorities. They will stamp it with visa."

"How much time that takes?" Natasha asked.

"Issuance of visa?" Mike enquired further.

"Yeah."

"About five days."

"Can it not be expedited? I am doing a job. I'll have to take leave from my office."

"We will try to expedite."

"And what about the Emirates card and bank account?"

"Oh, that can be applied on the same day and then you will be free. You can leave for India."

"Ok."

She stood up. Mike shook hands with her.

When she came out, she noticed two missed calls from Neelesh. She called back.

"Hello,"

"Natasha, where have you been?"

"I was in a meeting. Just got free."

"Are you aware we have not met in the last two days?"

"Yeah. I am sorry."

"Let us have dinner today."

Natasha thought for a moment. She, too, wanted a change. She said,

"Ok, where?"

"You can come to Vasant Kunj. We will decide after we meet."

"Right. I'll be reaching by nine."

They disconnected. After a while, her phone beeped. There was a message from Sukhdev. The pending VAT refund was sorted, the money would be transferred into the company's account in three days. She replied on the message itself. She smiled and thought that Sukhdev was quite efficient and he would not talk to his coworkers about how the things were managed.

* * *

Natasha boarded a flight from Dubai to New Delhi. It was after about a month of booking the apartment. She had to take leave from work for a week. She told Archit that she had to complete some of her father's pending work. On the other hand to Neelesh, she said she was in Dubai attending a CFO's conference.

She sat on her seat and thought half the work is done. She had got a residence visa in Dubai. She got an Emirates card and applied for a bank account in HSBC. This was done online. The other part of the work which is transferring the cash in US dollars to Dubai, she was confident that Sukhdev was capable of handling the same. She reclined on the seat and closed her eyes. She had to get rid of the money. Keeping the cash at home was like a live bomb and sharing the information with anyone was equally damaging. She had no choice.

Was Natasha joyful of this inheritance? No. That happiness was taken over by the fear of keeping such a massive stash of US currency at her house.

* * *

Neelesh observed that after her father's death, Natasha had changed. Something was amiss. He had checked about Advocate Vinod Goyal and found that he practised in Chandigarh. He was curious to know more about Vinod Goyal, so he dug deeper and found that Vinod Goyal was a setter. A setter is a person who believes in getting work done by managing the case by way of bribing the judge or the opposition's lawyer. He was, however, not sure why Natasha wanted to know about his credentials. She had said that one of her colleagues wanted to know about him.

Neelesh had his doubts.

* * *

Natasha resumed the office the next day. After the customary meeting with Archit, she came to her cabin and called Sukhdev. She said,

"Sukhdev, you should now contact the person who is going to transfer the money…"

"Mulliani?" Sukhdev asked.

"Yes, the same one."

"There would be no problem. Just tell me when the money will be transferred and where it will have to be transferred."

"Mulliani will be charging a commission?"

"Yes."

"How much?"

"Last time, we had paid one percent. I do not know what is the commission rate these days."

"Ok, ask him. If it is one percent, it is fine. We have already paid that much. If he demands more, then try to negotiate."

"I'll do that. I hope it shall not be more than one percent."

"Yes, one percent of this trade will be a lot of money in Indian currency."

"When and where, Madam."

"The money is to be transferred to Dubai. When? I'll let you know tomorrow. The money is yet to come to me."

Sukhdev knew it was company work and Natasha was not the sole authority. The senior management discussed such things and Natasha was just a channel. He said, "I'll go and talk to Mulliani."

He was about to stand up when Natasha signalled him to sit. She kept quiet for a few moments and then said,

"The transaction is a bit different this time."

Sukhdev listened intently. She continued,

"The cash this time is not in Indian currency. It is in US dollars and the amount is three million."

"You mean three million US dollars?"

"Yes," She continued,

"Do you think Mulliani will be able to handle it?"

Sukhdev smiled and said,

"Definitely, I'll talk to him today itself."

"No talking on the telephone either with Mulliani or with me. You know that."

"Yes, madam. Talks like these are always to be done in person."

"Good. If you need to talk to me about this, drop me a message and I'll tell you where we can meet."

"Sure," Sukhdev said and got up.

* * *

Ramesh Mulliani owned a big furniture store in the Kriti Nagar furniture market. Only a few people in his closed circle knew that Mulliani was engaged in Hawala transactions. The furniture shop was a façade. He used to earn more from the transfer of money compared to the sale of furniture. About eight employees were working in the shop. In addition to those eight employees, there was a manager named Ravi Chauhan. Ravi used to handle the customers. He used to manage the cash and hand over the accounts to Mulliani at the end of the day. Mulliani used to come to the shop daily for a couple of hours and would attend to the clients relating to his money-transferring business there only. He had a small corner office in the basement. He would come, sit there, make calls or attend to the clients from that office.

Sukhdev entered the shop. He was greeted by Ravi and directed to go downstairs. Sukhdev climbed the stairs and saw through the glass partition that Mulliani was sitting in his office. Sukhdev entered and smiled. They shook hands and sat down. They had met earlier, so there was no hesitation in initiating the talks. Mulliani asked,

"Company matters again."

"Yes, sir."

"How much this time?"

"Sir, what will be your fees?"

"You know it."

"Last time, you had charged one percent."

Mulliani smiled and said,

"When was it? It was perhaps three years back."

"Perhaps."

"It will be 1.5 percent."

"It will be substantial."

"You know my way of working. It is a hundred percent guaranteed. The fee I am quoting is quite reasonable. You hand over the money. Tell me the country where it is to be delivered and forget. It's my job."

"Yes, but I have to get confirmation from my boss. I don't know whether my boss will agree to 1.5 percent rate of commission. I have already told you charge one percent."

"You are trying to negotiate."

"Sort of. It's business."

"How much money is there and where will it be delivered? We can finalize the fee after knowing that."

"Three million US dollars, to be sent to Dubai."

"Three million US dollars? Mulliani wondered. It was a huge transaction. He said,

"That will be around twenty-one crores in Indian rupees."

"Yeah. Depending on the exchange rate, it is currently around seventy rupees to a dollar."

"You mean, you will hand over to me around twenty-one crore Indian Rupees and three million US dollars are to be handed over to the recipient in Dubai."

"No. I have three million US dollars right here. I'll be giving you that in cash."

"Oh, my god. It's a different and difficult proposal?"

"Why? I am making things easier for you. You would have got Indian rupees converted into US dollars before sending. I have cut down one step."

Mulliani leaned back on his chair, called a peon and asked him to bring tea. He kept quiet till the tea was served. He put his elbows on the table and leaned forward to speak slowly as if whispering,

"Mr Sukhdev, you don't understand our way of working. We don't physically transfer the money. I take money, Indian money and my counterpart in Dubai will hand over the currency in Dubai either in Dirham or in US dollars. We settle down accounts subsequently at regular intervals. What will I do with so much cash in US dollars."

Sukhdev was listening. He, however, said,

"That means it can't be done."

"It can be done, but then the dollars will have to be sent physically to Dubai."

"Through a courier?"

"One of my boys will carry it as passenger baggage and deliver it in Dubai."

"That sounds risky. Isn't it?"

"Tricky, yes. But that is why we charge a commission. I can guarantee the transfer that way, but the commission charges will be two percent."

"Sir, we were about to settle somewhere between one percent and one & half percent. Why two percent?"

"Had you given me Indian Rupees, we could still settle. Sending a boy with all precautions normally costs more."

"Have you sent the money through courier earlier?"

Mulliani laughed and said,

"A number of times, but this time it is three million dollars. That is a huge amount. You can tell your boss our commission will be set at two percent not a penny less."

"That will work out to be sixty thousand US dollars."

"You need not give me here. My counterpart in Dubai will hand over the money after deducting the commission."

"But what I am talking about is the quantum. You have to reconsider the percentage of your commission. It's a request. My boss may ask for another person for the job, but I trust you completely."

"Then go and convince your boss."

"Please sir, there is room for negotiation in all businesses."

"You seem to be a hard negotiator."

"Sir, a hard negotiator is always a good paymaster. He will never cheat."

"First, you go and have a meeting with your boss. Convey everything. I am sure whosoever is your boss will agree."

Sukhdev looked dejected. He stood up and said,

"Sir, please consider fifty thousand US dollars. I'll convince my boss."

Mulliani again laughed and said,

"Ok, you arrange for the money. We may settle somewhere between fifty and sixty."

Sukhdev got up. They shook hands. Sukhdev went out. Mulliani saw him going upstairs. He had some thoughts. He called him back and said,

"I have to ask one thing."

"Yes." Sukhdev got curious.

"The money has nothing to do with terrorism?"

"What are you saying?"

Mulliani could see a shocking reaction on Sukhdev's face. He was shrewd enough to judge.

"Why did you ask?" Sukhdev said.

"No. Nothing. Since it is a big amount. It just came to my mind. Don't worry. Call me or inform me when you intend to visit. We will meet here."

"Yes, sir. I'll call before coming."

_ * * * *

Chapter - V

Natasha was in her Gurugram apartment. Sukhdev had just left after narrating the exchange he had with Mulliani. She poured a drink for herself and sat down on the bed. Physically carrying the cash outside India might be risky, but she was not privy to Mulliani's modus operandi. However, she was worried the quantum was huge. Should it be sent in one go or two/three instalments? She was not sure. She had recently visited Dubai and learnt that the baggage allowance was capped at two checked-in bags, each of 23 kgs per traveller for most careers, except Air India, which allowed up to 30 kg.

She took out the phone, googled it and found out the weight of one $100 bill was almost one gm. That meant the total weight of the cash she had lying around would be 30 kg. She figured out that if those were to be sent in one go, whosoever would be the carrier would require two suitcases. Assuming the person was to fly Air India, there was the suitcase's weight, and the money would be hidden by some clothes etc. Regarding volume, it might be challenging to fit all the cash in one suitcase.

She had asked Sukhdev to bargain for the commission to pretend it was the company's matter. She otherwise was inclined to part with the amount. Her interest was the smooth transfer of the money. She had asked Sukhdev to have one more meeting with Mulliani to confirm how Mulliani would deliver the money in Dubai.

She looked around the room. She didn't have suitcases big enough to carry that much cash. Though it was for Mulliani to figure out, the cash had to be delivered to him. She would never risk asking Mulliani to come to her place.

In a day or two, that job had to be taken care of.

Natasha hadn't finished her drink when the bell rang. She was not expecting anyone. Curiously, she got up and looked at the hole. It was Neelesh. She opened the door and said,

"Hey, how come. It's a surprise!"

"Yes, long time."

"How did you know I am here at Gurugram?"

"Simple. You know both the drivers are friends. They work like spies."

Both laughed. Neelesh came forward and hugged her. She asked for a drink, pointing towards her drink.

"What's a hurry? I am here to spend the night."

"No. That is not possible."

"Why?"

Natasha smiled and said, "There are spies downstairs."

"Oh, I forgot. But they know we keep on meeting."

"Still, if you intend to stay here, let them off duty. Tell them you will drop me at my Dwarka house later. I have some work tomorrow at that place."

"Tomorrow? It is the weekend?"

"I know. Lot of work is to be done."

"Ok, madam."

Natasha called Kuku and told him to go to her Dwarka apartment and park the car there. Kuku was briefed about the next morning's schedule. Neelesh went downstairs and came up with his briefcase.

* * *

Natasha was at the Vasant Kunj Mall when Sukhdev called her. She asked him to meet her at the mall. While window shopping, she saw a shop displaying luggage bags and entered it. She was looking for suitcases with a number lock. There were brands of American Tourister, Samsonite, VIP, Safari, etc. The VIP suitcases were comparatively cheaper but the colours could have been more comfortable. It was light blue. She asked the salesman for a darker shade. Those were available in other brands.

Meanwhile, her phone beeped. It was Sukhdev. She asked him to wait at **Starbucks**. Natasha came out without purchasing the suitcases. Sukhdev was waiting. She joined him.

"Good afternoon, madam," Sukhdev greeted.

"Good afternoon. What happened?" Natasha enquired.

"Mulliani had agreed to do the job at fifty-five thousand US dollars."

"Ok," she said and looked at him questioningly. Sukhdev continued.

"Mulliani says that once the money reaches his counterpart. He will be given a code and the same code will be given to the recipient at Dubai. The recipient can collect the money from the said person on disclosing the code."

Natasha smiled and said,

"It looks as if we are smugglers."

"In a way, yes," said Sukhdev. He continued, "But that is how their systems work. It is completely based on trust. No documents. Nothing mentioned anywhere."

Natasha thought that Sukhdev was right in a way; she was smuggling the money out of India. She said,

"When do we need to deliver the cash?"

"That is for us to see."

"Can we do it tomorrow?"

"Tomorrow is a Sunday. Yes, it can be done.

"Will he collect, or shall we deliver?"

"Better we deliver."

"Exactly. I was thinking along the same lines."

"I will talk to Archit, sir. I think the cash is ready. I will call you tomorrow and ask you to come from where it is to be collected."

"You will be there?"

"Yes. Yes, definitely. No third person knows about it," said Natasha.

"Ok, Madam," Sukhdev got up and went out.

Natasha went to the same bag shop and purchased two light blue suitcases from VIP. The smaller one went inside, the bigger one, and when she walked out of the store, it looked like she was carrying one suitcase.

* * *

On Sunday, after the domestic help left, Natasha took the polybags from the bed and placed the bunch of US dollars neatly and carefully in one suitcase. Fifteen bunches of 10 racks of US dollars in one suitcase and, 15 bunches of 10 racks of US dollars in another were placed. There was still some space left in both the suitcases. She filled that space with old newspapers. She locked both suitcases at code 333. She called Kuku and asked him to put the suitcases in the car. She was headed to her flat in Gurugram.

When she sat in the car, for the first time in her life, she felt fear and guilt. She was doing an illegal work. The car was full of three million US dollars and she was sitting there.

It was frightful.

Kuku brought both the suitcases upstairs at Natasha's Gurugram house. She had asked Sukhdev to be at her place by 1 pm. She had not had her breakfast. However, she had brought a few vegetable sandwiches with her. She looked at her watch. It was 12:30 pm. Still, half an hour was there. She opened the packet and started eating the sandwich. She had a feeling as if she couldn't taste a thing. At 12:50 pm, she called Kuku and sent him to the market on an errand. She wanted Kuku to be away, particularly when Sukhdev would take the suitcases. Though Kuku was reliable, it was the strong feeling of guilt that compelled her to send Kuku away.

When Sukhdev came, Natasha asked him to count the money. Sukhdev said,

"It's fine, madam, if you have counted."

"It is always appropriate. Mulliani would also count the same. You must be sure about the quantum."

She opened the suitcases by arranging the lock at 333. Sukhdev counted the bunches, made some calculations on paper and rearranged the cash in both suitcases. Natasha said,

"Remember the lock code. It is 333 in both the suitcases."

"Ok, madam."

"Now give that piece of paper to me on which you have made calculations," Natasha said.

He handed over the piece of paper and said,

"I will take these directly to Mulliani and once handed over, our job is over."

Natasha smiled and said,

"Yes, hopefully."

Sukhdev carried both suitcases away from Natasha's apartment. Natasha was looking from the side of the window, that he was keeping both suitcases in the back of his car. She kept watching till he drove past the exit.

* * *

Mulliani had in the past physically transported cash in US dollars out of India, but the highest amount sent was $500,000. Typically, it was $100,000. Only once was it $500,000. This time he was taking a big risk. The commission was big, too. Fifty-five thousand US dollars means around 40 lakhs Indian Rupees. He was confident that there wouldn't be any problem. He was in this business for many years. He was known to have never made a mistake. He was known to have never cheated any client. The business works on trust. One failure meant it was gone.

Mulliani used three boys out of his eight employees in the furniture shop for this work. Prince, Nihal and Jaydev were his most confidants. They were sent abroad one at a time on the pretext of meeting the suppliers for the import of furniture. He decided to send Nihal to Dubai to talk to Rashid in Dubai. Rashid originally belonged to Bangladesh and had settled in Dubai. He lived in Deira and was in the business of money transfers. Such money transfer in Dubai was not illegal. Rashid was told that Nihal would be coming with the consignment.

He checked the airline schedule and decided to book Nihal on Air India Express. The flight was the next day, Monday at 11.20 pm. It was a direct flight.

After the work shift was over, he asked Nihal to stay back. Around 9 pm, all the others had left and only Mulliani and Nihal stayed. Mulliani told Nihal, "Tomorrow night, you are flying to Dubai."

"Sir."

"You will have two suitcases containing US dollars and will hand over these to Rashid."

Nihal had carried the US dollars on earlier occasions in handbags. He asked,

"Two suitcases mean those will have to be checked in."

"Yes."

"Sir, it appears to be a big consignment."

"Yes, you must know it will have three million US dollars."

Nihal's eyes widened."

"That much!"

"Yes. But I am taking all precautions. I'll pack it properly. There will be layers of your garments over the currency. Once these are checked in here at Delhi Airport, the risk, if any, would be over. At Dubai Airport, nobody bothers."

"Sir…" Nihal was about to say something when Mulliani interrupted.

"Nihal, you will be suitably compensated. I know it's a big job. But I promise you will never regret it."

"Thank you, sir."

"Flight will be at 11:20 pm tomorrow. You can reach there by 8 pm to have sufficient time for check-in."

"Ok."

"Tomorrow morning, you can come to the shop as usual. Bring some of your garments in a bag and leave them in my cabin. Then you can go. Prince and Jaydev will meet you at the airport. They will hand over the suitcases and tickets there. You reach there with your passport."

"What about the visa?"

"I have talked to Rashid. It will come online tomorrow. I have a scanned copy of your passport and photograph. It has already been sent to Rashid."

"Will the visa come in a day?"

"That is Rashid's job. He will do. He has done earlier, too."

"But suppose...."

Mulliani smiled and said,

"Don't worry, if it gets delayed, we will postpone the trip."

"Right, sir."

Nihal went out. Mulliani was thinking that Nihal might be right. The visa would have to be ensured. He called Rashid. Rashid laughed and said the visa would be sent by 2:30 pm India time.

* * * * *

Chapter - VI

It was Monday. Early in the morning, Neelesh had to leave for Chandigarh. He had a matter listed for hearing at the High Court of Punjab and Haryana (P & H High Court). It was a five-hour drive. The courts usually start at 10:30 am. He left at 5 am from Delhi. Kishan was driving. His client was the manufacturer of electrical appliances with the brand name ALTARA. However, some other people claimed the brand ALTARA was registered under his name. He had filed a petition praying that Neelesh's client be restrained from using the brand name ALTARA.

The advocate on the opposite side was Vinod Goyal. The matter was listed before a single-member bench. At around noon, their matter came up for hearing. Vinod Goyal started arguing.

Vinod said, "My lord, my client is the registered owner of the ALTARA brand for the class of goods covering electrical appliances. Here is the copy of the certificate."

He passed on the copy to the Judge. Vinod continued.

"It came to the knowledge of my client that one M/s Kenmore Pvt. Ltd. Is using the brand name ALTARA, which is an infringement. As the rightful owner, my client had never given any rights or permission to Kenmore Pvt. Ltd. To use the brand name ALTARA. The application before your lordship is for restraining Kenmore Pvt. Ltd. From using the said brand name."

The Judge looked at the papers lying before him. He read the applicants' grounds. After a while, he lifted his head, looked at Neelesh and said,

"You, representing M/s Kenmore Pvt. Ltd?"

"Yes, my lord," responded Neelesh.

Neelesh continued, "He says his client is the registered owner of the brand, so how come your client is using the same? Mr Vinod Goyal had produced the registration certificate issued by the Trade Mark Act, 1999."

"Lordship, I have seen the certificate. I am producing my application before the Trade Mark Authority, which was made prior to their application. Mr Goyal's client made the application two years after my client made the application. My client is using the brand name ALTARA much earlier than their application. Lordship, I am wondering why the status of my application is being shown on the website as 'pending'. How come the application filed at a later date has been considered and was duly registered."

Vinod Goyal got up and said,

"Lordship, yes, it is a fact on record that Kenmore Pvt. Ltd. had made an application on an earlier date, but the Trade Mark Authority must have taken cognizance of same. They would have found defects in the application or the declarations or those may not be proper."

The judge was listening. Vinod Goyal continued,

"The presumption is always that Kenmore Pvt. Ltd.'s application was defective and that is the reason, the brand name was assigned to my client."

The judge smiled and looked at Neelesh. Neelesh said,

"My lord, even if the presumption is correct, my client should have been put to notice intimating or pointing out the faults, if any. Moreover, the website doesn't say that it has been rejected. It says that it is still pending."

The Judge looked again at the papers lying before him for a few minutes and asked the stenographer to write the judgement. The matter was referred to the Trade Mark Authority with the directions to look into both applications afresh and till that time, the status quo would be maintained. That means both the claimants of a brand name could continue to use ALTARA.

Both Vinod Goyal and Neelesh collected their respective papers and came out.

Vinod Goyal said to Neelesh,

"You are perhaps not from Chandigarh?"

"I came from Delhi," Neelesh replied.

"I am Vinod." He said and extended his hand.

"Neelesh here." They shook hands.

"We have a good canteen here in the High Court. If you are not in a hurry, we can have coffee," Vinod suggested.

Neelesh agreed. They went to the canteen and settled down. It was full of fellow lawyers. Vinod asked the canteen boy for two teas and some sandwiches.

"So, how is practice?" Vinod asked.

"Earlier, it was better. Nowadays, there are a smaller number of cases."

"Same here."

"Justice Somesh Chowdhary was here in P & H High Court. He retired about six months back."

"Yes. I heard he passed away a couple of months back?"

"Yeah."

"He was a nice, very nice judge."

"Have you appeared before him?"

"Yes, number of times. I remember he was about to retire and I had appeared two days before his retirement."

"Was he liberal? Some judges tend not to give favourable orders, even if the merit is there. Some are known as liberal, who give reasoned judgements if a case is strong on its merits."

"Oh, yes, he was liberal."

"An upright and honest person."

"Yeah," Vinod said, but he stammered, and for the first time, he realized why they had unnecessarily drifted to Justice Chowdhary."

"How did you manage to get the brand name registered?" Neelesh asked.

"Oh. This case. It's not difficult. Money plays a big role."

"I have heard that your client is neither a trader nor a manufacturer; where is he using the brand name ALTARA."

Vinod laughed and said,

"It's a game. Some people earn money like this."

"I didn't follow you," Neelesh replied.

Vinod elaborated, "Look, your client, Kenmore Pvt. Ltd., is a big manufacturer. Their goods are being sold in the brand ALTARA. If they are told they cannot use ALTARA tomorrow, their sales will be reduced to a large extent."

"That's right. But what does your client gain?"

"You are not a novice. Kenmore Pvt. Ltd., will have to approach my client and my client would be offered a big amount running into crores. There is no option and my client will readily sell the brand name in exchange of money."

"That is his business?" Neelesh asked.

"Yes. It is his business."

"And people like you help him?"

"He is my client. I am his lawyer. I have to defend his interest."

"Isn't it strange?"

"That is the way the world goes."

"Which was the last case where you appeared before Justice Chowdhary?"

Vinod kept quiet for a few minutes and said,

"All judgements are available on the High Court's website."

He got up and said,

"Thank you, sir. It was nice to meet you. I have another matter post-lunch session."

Neelesh looked at the watch. It was time to leave for Delhi.

* * *

At 3 pm on Monday, Sukhdev got a message from Mulliani the consignment would be sent that night. Sukhdev came to Natasha's cabin and knocked. She said, "Yes, come in."

"Madam, the consignment will be sent tonight. Mulliani just sent me a message," Sukhdev informed.

"Are you careful while texting him?"

"Of course, Madam."

"So, we will get the confirmation by tomorrow morning."

"Yes, madam."

Sukhdev smiled and went out.

* * *

Mulliani had opened both the suitcases, repacked the cash in a polythene paper and wrapped it with sellotape. The cash was placed at the bottom of the suitcases and covered it with old and used clothes. He locked these and moved the numbers randomly. The visa had arrived, printouts taken and the ticket on Air India were booked. It was a big consignment. He was also apprehensive and wanted to take no chances. He called Prince and Jaydev. Both the suitcases were lying in one corner of his office. He asked both of them to sit down. He addressed to both,

"There is an important assignment for both of you. Here are two suitcases." Mulliani pointed towards the suitcases and continued.

"Nihal is going to take these to Dubai tonight. He will reach the airport departure at 8 pm. The flight is at 11:20 pm. You can take a cab and reach the airport around 8 pm. Handover these suitcases to Nihal."

Mulliani opened his drawer and took out a few papers. He said, "This is the ticket and visa for Dubai. Give these to Nihal."

"Ok, sir," Prince said.

"Is there any difficulty?" Mulliani asked.

"No. Not at all." Prince said. Jaydev nodded in unison.

"What is the time now?"

"7 pm"

"It will take you one hour to reach?"

"Little less. Maybe 40-45 minutes," Jaydev said.

"No problem. You can leave now. Call Nihal and coordinate. You keep it on a baggage trolley outside the airport. Nihal will take it from there."

"It will be done, sir," Prince said.

"One more thing. Tell Nihal that both of you will be waiting outside the airport. Once the suitcases are checked in, Nihal should come near the exit gate where you will be standing. Ask him to wave at you with his boarding pass. You both will stay at the airport till the flight has departed. It will be displayed on the board."

"Sure, sir. We are not doing it for the first time."

Mulliani smiled and said, "Yes, I know, but it is just a precaution, and I am in the habit of repeating it every time."

Both Prince and Jaydev took the suitcases and left.

* * *

Nihal, too, was fully aware of the procedure. He had got a call from Prince; they had left for the airport and might be reaching a little before 8 pm. He hired a cab carrying nothing except his passport.

* * *

Natasha had called Neelesh after she came out of the office. Neelesh was on his way back to Delhi. Neelesh told her he would reach Delhi a bit late and said they could meet the next day. Natasha, however, was thinking if the money would reach Dubai the next day, she would have to go to Dubai for a day to receive it. She decided to take a flight on Tuesday night or Wednesday morning. She would collect the money and deposit it in her HSBC account in Dubai.

Chapter - VII

On Monday, at 5 pm, she came out of a classroom after her lecture to probationers on money laundering. Walking briskly through the corridor, she entered the last room on the left side. Outside the room, it said Ameya Mohite, Joint Director. She put the papers and a folder on the table, asked the peon for a cup of tea and looked at her watch. She still had an hour before the day ended. Ameya was 48 years old and the joint director at the Enforcement Directorate (ED). She was always happy to volunteer herself for lectures to trainees and probationers.

The peon brought the tea. As she was sipping the tea, a knock was at the door. It was Raghunath, the Assistant Director.

"Come, come, Raghunath," she said.

"We have received a tip from an informer that a big consignment of foreign currency is being sent through a passenger to Dubai."

"Who is the informer? Is he reliable?"

"Yes, his last two tips were up to the mark."

"What exactly has he shared?" Ameya asked without showing much interest. The directorate got such calls every day and most of them were bogus.

"The informer told the passenger's name, the flight number and the amount."

"How much is the amount?"

"Three million US dollars?"

Ameya was about to drop the cup.

"What?"

"Yes, madam. It is unbelievable."

"Who sends money like that these days? There are various other methods and we keep on investigating those. Sending that much cash through a passenger is old-fashioned and crude."

"That is what the informer shared."

"Which flight?"

"Air India Express leaving at 11.20 pm tonight."

Ameya kept thinking for a while. She was accustomed to such calls, but the amount was huge. She said,

"Let us take a chance. Hopefully, your informer is correct."

"Yes, madam."

"I may be leaving in another hour. You make a team of five officers. You will be leading the team."

"Sure, madam."

"And keep me informed."

Raghunath came out of Ameya's room and went to his room. Raghunath picked up the phone and asked Samir to come to his room. Samir was a senior intelligence officer (SIO), quite active and energetic. He belonged to Lucknow and got married recently. Samir came to Raghunath's room.

"Samir, please take the chair," Raghunath said. Samir sat down.

"We have received a tip. Make a team of five officers. You can take four IOs. I will be accompanying."

Samir seemed reluctant,

"Sir, I had promised my wife for a dinner at some good place. If you can do it without me."

Raghunath, as if expecting the response, said.

"No. You are to be part of this team. It is important."

Raghunath smiled and spoke.

"Samir, I know you are newly married and have obligations towards your wife. You should have. But you haven't heard what the tip is."

"What, sir?"

"Three million US dollars."

"In cash?"

"Yes. The informer says the amount is being carried by the passenger in baggage."

"Sir, don't you think it is bogus? Who carries so much cash these days?"

"But the informer is quite sure. I have already talked to Ameya madam. She has permitted to proceed."

"You said the flight departure time is 11:20 pm. They open the check-in counters about three hours before, say 8:20 pm."

"Some airlines open four hours before the flight time. There is a possibility the passenger will check in as early as possible as that much cash cannot be carried in a handbag. There must be one checked–in bag or maybe two."

"That means we should be at the airport around 7:20 pm."

"Yes, what do we know about the passenger?"

"We know the passenger's name and flight number."

Samir looked at his watch and said, "It's 5:30 pm now. We have an hour to leave."

"Yes, please organize the team and don't forget to call your wife. Tell her about the compelling circumstances."

Samir got up, looked at his senior dryly and left the room.

* * *

At around 7:30 pm, a team of enforcement officers led by Raghunath, the Assistant Director, was inside the departure hall of terminal 3 of the IGI Airport in New Delhi. There was a crowd of passengers at almost all rows. The Air India flights were managed at row A. The counters were open. Samir approached the lady sitting at one of the counters. He talked to her and she directed Samir to a small room at the backside of the counter. Samir went inside and met the shift supervisor. He introduced himself and checked the Air India express flight manifest, which was scheduled for 11.30 pm. The name Nihal Singh was there. He enquired from the supervisor whether the checking-in had started. He said it had not been announced, though a few passengers had already lined up at the counters. Samir told the supervisor that he was looking for a particular person and he should be informed when the passenger reported at the counter. Samir also cautioned the supervisor to be discreet and that there should be no lapse. The supervisor was an experienced official. He assured Samir and told him to be near the counters only.

Samir came out and briefed Raghunath. The other four officers got scattered near the Air India counters. The time was around 8 pm.

* * *

Prince and Jaydev had reached outside the airport departure gate, unloaded both suitcases and placed those on a baggage trolley. Nihal was yet to arrive. There were a lot of passengers with loaded trolleys standing outside the airport departure gates. As usual, they were talking and saying goodbyes to their friends or relatives who had come to drop them off. In another ten minutes, they saw Nihal walking towards them, smiling. The three met. Nihal looked at the trolley and the two light blue suitcases. He placed it on the trolley and asked, "Are these the suitcases?"

"Yes, from here onwards, it is your job. We were responsible for safe transportation up to this point," Prince said.

Nihal laughed and said,

"Oh yes. Don't worry, and where are my ticket and visa?"

"I forgot. Here they are." Prince said, taking out the papers from the inner pocket of his coat. The time was 8.15 pm.

Nihal, got hold of the trolley and was about to move when Prince said quickly,

"Nihal when you complete the check-in and get the boarding pass, just come near gate no. 5 and wave at us. We would be here till that time."

"Sure," Nihal said standing in the line for security personnel to verify the ticket and passport. Once it was done, Nihal waved at them and went inside. Once inside, he looked at the board displaying row numbers. Air India was at row A.

* * *

Raghunath had strictly asked the officers not to check the passport of any passenger at random because that might get noticed by the suspect. The officers were just to roam around Air-India counters and wait for the suspect to report at the counter. Air India opened the check-in and the passengers were reporting one by one. There were three counters earmarked for Air India Express flight departing for Dubai. It was displayed on the monitors installed over each counter.

Samir was watching for a male passenger carrying two suitcases. Two suitcases were not there in the information but it was safely presumed the quantum of cash mentioned could not be carried in one suitcase. Samir noticed that almost all the passengers were carrying two suitcases. Very few passengers were carrying one suitcase.

Nihal looked at the watch. It was 8.40 pm and there was a long queue. He was holding his trolley with two suitcases. The staff at the counters were working slowly. They seemed to be in no hurry. There were still more than two-and-half hours. Most of the passengers in the queue looked like construction labours. There is a huge migration of construction workers from India entering into employment in the UAE. The queue was moving gradually. After standing in the queue for half an hour, Nihal reached near the counter. Two passengers were ahead of him. Many more had joined the queue behind him. He saw one of the passengers being escorted by airline staff towards the corner. Nihal was aware that some of the names on the passenger's list were marked for random checking and the airline staff had the instructions that such passengers, along with the baggage, were to be brought to customs staff before check-in. He had such an experience once before but luckily; he was not carrying anything suspicious on that occasion. He was signalled by the lady sitting at the counter. He immediately pushed his trolley and reached there. He produced his passport and ticket. The lady there examined the passport, looked at his face and scanned his passport. The supervisor sitting in his cabin was watching in his system. He immediately got up and came out. Samir was standing near the counter. The supervisor briskly walked to him and whispered. Raghunath was watching both of them from a distance. It appeared the suspect had reported. He signalled to other officers. Meanwhile, Samir walked towards Nihal. He asked the lady to hand over the passport. Samir looked at the name. He asked him,

"What's your name?"

"Nihal Singh, sir."

"Any baggage?"

Nihal kept mum. Samir asked again.

"Are you carrying any baggage?" Nihal pointed towards the trolley and said,

"Yes, these two suitcases."

"Come with me."

"Is there a problem, sir?"

"Can you please come with me?"

Nihal, holding the trolley, started walking with him. Once both of them were away from row A, more persons joined. These all were from the Enforcement Directorate. Nihal could smell that there was going to be a big problem.

All of them entered the room of the customs officer. Raghunath introduced himself, showed his ID and informed that they needed his room for some time. The customs officer nodded. Raghunath asked one of his officers to stay outside the door to guard. It was Samir who started talking.

"So, Nihal Singh, where are you going?"

"Dubai."

"Do you work there?"

"No, sir, I am going on a tourist visa."

"With so much baggage, two suitcases."

"Yes, sir."

"Is there someone else travelling with you?"

"I am going alone."

"What do you do?"

"Sir, I work a job at a furniture shop."

"In Delhi?"

"Yes, sir, in Kirti Nagar."

"How much money do you draw as salary?"

"Rs twenty-five thousand."

"Per month?"

"Yes sir."

"Do you know how much is the cost of a ticket to Dubai?"

"No sir, I was going to meet a supplier in Dubai. My employer bought the ticket and arranged for the visa."

"Who is your employer?"

"Ramesh Mulliani."

Raghunath was listening. Mulliani's name had appeared sometimes in profiling. Raghunath was more interested in opening the suitcases. He intercepted,

"How much currency are you carrying?"

"Currency?"

"Yes," Raghunath said in a harsh tone.

"One hundred dollars," Nihal said, taking out a bill of one hundred dollars."

"What is in these suitcases?"

"My clothes."

"Liar. Two suitcases full of your clothes. Open these."

Nihal was nervous and he started stammering. Samir pushed Nihal towards the trolley and said,

"Unlock these?"

"Sir, please listen…"

Samir took the suitcases from the trolley and examined them. Those had number locks. He pointed towards Nihal and said,

"What's the code?" Nihal kept silent. One of the officers slapped him and said,

"What's the number?"

"I don't know, sir," Nihal said with tears in his eyes.

Raghunath said, "If you do not cooperate with us, we will have no choice but to break it. We need to see the contents and if there is nothing objectionable, there is still time for the flight to go."

Nihal stood confused. He finally admitted,

"Sir, these suitcases were given to me in a locked situation. I don't know the number."

"Then we have to break the lock," Samir said.

The officers had the tools with them. They were anticipating such a situation. Two IOs started working on the locks randomly and when they were unable to unlock, they took out the tools from their pockets. It took them about 25 minutes to break the lock of both the suitcases. The first suitcase was opened. It had clothes. Samir took out the clothes. There was nothing underneath. He took out everything and examined the bottom of the suitcase, looking for some false cavity. No. He found nothing. He looked at Raghunath, and Samir opened another suitcase. There were old clothes. He took those out and at the bottom was one envelope. He opened it. In hand, ten thousand US dollars. That meant only one rack of 100 dollar bills. Samir further examined the bottom of the second suitcase carefully. Nothing was there. He found no scope of hidden cavities.

Samir stood up. Raghunath and Samir silently looked at each other.

* * * * *

Chapter - VIII

Waiting outside gate no. 5, Prince and Jaydev were getting restless and continuously trying to look for Nihal. Nihal was yet to appear as per plan. Nor was he seen anywhere in the crowd and two hours had passed. Jaydev had made two rounds around all departure gates, but Nihal hadn't shown up as planned. The check-in was 30-45 minutes job. Prince looked at his watch. It was 10:15 pm. He called Mulliani.

"Sir,"

"Yes, where are you?"

"Sir, we are still at the airport. Nihal was supposed to come near the gate and give us the signal after checking in, but he did not. Nor can he be seen anywhere."

"At what time he had entered."

"Almost two hours have passed."

Mulliani, on the other end, got anxious; Nihal could not forget about the signal. It was a standard practice. The negative thoughts started coming in. Had the customs officers nabbed him?"

"Sir?" Asked Prince.

"You keep waiting. There is still time for the flight to leave. I hope Nihal will show himself."

"Ok, sir."

Both of them had no other option but to wait. Mulliani was almost sure something had gone wrong. The amount involved was huge. If a problem occurred, his reputation would be at stake. He had always succeeded in delivering so far.

* * *

Raghunath stood dumbfounded. It was his informant. Ameya was reluctant. Samir was reluctant. They both were of the view no one carries cash like this anymore. He came out of the room and called his informer. He could hear the ringtone on the other side. No one answered. He disconnected. Samir, too, joined him. He said, "Sir, it happens. It has happened on many previous occasions. The tips are not always hundred percent correct, but looking at the amount of cash involved. We had to take a chance…"

"No, no, Samir, this informer has never been wrong. He is part of one such syndicate. They are aware of other operations."

Raghunath was holding the phone in his hand when there was a ring. It was the informer. He got up and walked a little away from Samir.

"You are wrong," Raghunath said. He continued, "He only had ten thousand dollars on him, not three million, as you had shared."

"Sir, it is not possible. I am sure the suitcases were stuffed with three million dollars."

"Oh, stop. The passenger is in front of us, both suitcases are lying open and this is what we have found."

"Sir, you have verified the passenger's identity?"

"Do you think we are doing this job for the first time? We verified everything and he refers to Ramesh Mulliani as his employer."

"That's right. Nihal is Mulliani's man. Sir, the money has to be there."

Raghunath disconnected the phone angrily. He walked towards Samir and said,

"It was the informer. He is still sticking to three million."

Samir didn't listen and said,

"Sir, please call Ameya madam and appraise her."

"Yeah, she has to be told. But I still cannot distrust my informer. This man, Nihal, seems to have played some trick. What to do with Nihal? Shall we allow him to go?"

"But sir, carrying ten thousand dollars is also an offence. We have to take action against him."

"What action?"

"Sir, by now, everyone at the airport, airline staff, customs and police have come to know that six people from the Enforcement Directorate are here. Our presence in this strength indicates that we were anticipating a big catch. We cannot allow him to go. At least the amount of ten thousand dollars has to be detained. His statement will have to be recorded."

"What shall I tell Ameya madam?" Raghunath said.

"Sir, tell her the information was not correct and the amount that has been recovered. Tell her we are bringing the person to our office for interrogation."

"Yeah, but detention has to be made here. Ask an Intelligence Officer (IO) to prepare the papers and request the customs officers to arrange for two witnesses. Meanwhile, I am going to talk to Ameya madam."

Samir went inside the customs room and Raghunath called Ameya. She quickly responded. Raghunath narrated the complete sequence of events. Ameya kept listening, patiently. She finally said, "Prepare the *Panchnama* (recovery memo) at the airport itself because the recovery has been made there. Be quick. Don't take more than half an hour. Avoid wasting time. Bring the person along with you at the office. In the morning, we will see what has to be done with him."

"Right, madam," Raghunath said. He was relaxed a bit because Ameya didn't get furious.

* * *

It was 11.30 pm now. However, the notice board had still not declared the Air India Express flight to Dubai as 'departed.' Prince and Jaydev were sure that something wrong had happened to Nihal. Mulliani had not called them. As both were discussing the further course of action, Jaydev exclaimed.

"Oh, look, Nihal is being pushed in that car."

Prince looked. Two cars were parked near gate no. 1 on the first lane meant for buses. Two persons were seen loading the suitcases in one of the vehicles. They were quick and the two cars drove past them, in a couple of minutes. Prince saw Nihal sitting on the back seat with two people on Nihal's side.

Prince and Jaydev were sure that Nihal had been taken in custody or would be arrested. Prince immediately called Mulliani,

"Sir, I have bad news. It appears Nihal has been apprehended."

"How do you know?" Mulliani asked.

"We just saw Nihal being pushed in a car. Two cars and maybe four or five persons taking him away."

"Were they in uniform?"

"No."

Mulliani thought for a moment and said,

"Listen carefully, I am switching off my phone. Don't try to call me, I'll reach out. Both of you must resume your duties at the shop tomorrow, as usual. You don't know anything about what happened tonight. Understand?"

"Yes, sir."

"Now go away quickly."

Mulliani switched off his phone. He was still at the shop alone, waiting to hear from them. He looked around. He knew that there should not be anything objectionable found in his office. He was always careful. He opened his drawer. There was another mobile phone with a different sim card he obtained long back on a bogus identity. He switched on the second phone. It was not charged. He put it on a charger. It had to be charged. He had to wait. Staying longer in the shop was risky. However, he was sure that nothing would happen in another hour. When the phone was charged about 50 percent, he picked up the phone and the charger. He came out. A guard was sitting outside. Mulliani signalled him to close the shutter. He sat down in the car and drove towards Ravi Chauhan's home, his manager. The time was 12.10 am. He spoke to Ravi for a few minutes near the door and rushed away.

* * *

Raghunath and Samir were sitting in one car, and all the others, including Nihal, were in the second car. The total driving time from the airport to the Enforcement Directorate at night would be 30 minutes. Samir was driving. Raghunath said,

"What do you think? What could have happened?"

Samir smiled and said,

"Sir, please don't mind, but the information was incorrect on the face of it. We have seen this happen before."

"Yes, but presuming the informer is correct. Two suitcases full of cash of three million dollars were handed over to Nihal by Mulliani. What other possibilities could be there?"

"Sir, you still believe the informer was correct?"

"Yes."

"Sir, the only possibilities are either Mulliani had bad intentions and wanted to grab the money or Nihal made some mischief on his way to the airport. Nihal pulling mischief on the way was practically not possible. Moreover, he knows that cheating a boss like Mulliani means inviting trouble. These are all syndicates. These people can easily get him killed. What I think is, if your informer is correct, Nihal has nothing to do with it. He must have been handed over the two suitcases in the presence of a client under the pretext that he will transport the three million dollars."

Raghunath was quiet. At this point, he didn't know whether Samir was right or wrong. But he agreed that it was highly improbable for Nihal to change the suitcase or substitute the contents. Samir looked at his senior and asked, "You don't seem to agree with me?"

"No. It's not that. You have correctly analyzed. I will meet the informer in person and talk to him. It might give me an idea of how authentic he is."

"Shall I accompany you, sir?"

"No. It's always better to meet the informer alone."

"That's right, sir."

"I fail to understand why the informer would quote the figure of three million. He must have heard or seen it. He cannot quote such a figure out of the blue. There must be some truth in that."

"Sir, if there is any truth in what he had told, the money is here somewhere."

"That needed to be tracked."

"Sir. I'll drop you at the office and then, can I go home? My wife is waiting. I've already received three messages from her."

Raghunath smiled and said,

"Sure, just drop me and go. I will depute two IOs to take charge of Nihal. But be in the office tomorrow morning by 9:30 am. We will debrief Ameya madam and decide the further course of action."

"Sir, Nihal has to be interrogated?"

"Yes, definitely, we may get some lead."

"When do you intend to meet the informer?"

"I'll try to meet him early in the morning, so that when we talk with Ameya madam, I have more clarity."

In another ten minutes, both cars reached the office of the Enforcement Directorate. Everyone got down. Nihal was taken inside. The two suitcases followed him. Raghunath shook hands with Samir and entered the building. Samir sat in his car and texted his wife that he would reach home in another 20 minutes.

* * * * *

Chapter - IX

Mulliani had checked in at a budget hotel in Ghaziabad, Uttar Pradesh and called his wife from there. For the time being, it was safe, but he knew that once the investigation would pick up steam, he would have to find some other hideout. Ghaziabad was near Delhi and it was easier for him to keep an eye on what was happening to Nihal. He now knew the people who took Nihal away from the airport were from the ED. He resisted calling his source at the directorate. He worried about what he would tell Sukhdev. He must be trying his number. It would convey a wrong message not only to Sukhdev but to all his clients and other operators. He had to plan his moves intellegently.

Mulliani's wife's parents stayed in Jaipur. He sent her there for a few weeks to keep her out of all this. He had told his wife everything. At about 8 am, he arranged for a cab and sent his wife off to Jaipur.

He preferred to use the hotel's phone. First, he called Rashid and told him everything. Rashid wondered about Nihal. He was expecting Nihal at his place with the money early in the morning. Mulliani assured Rashid that he was trying to find out what had happened and was naturally worried about handing over the money. Rashid was a rich man. The transaction of dollars in cash in Dubai was otherwise legal. Rashid assured him that if the need arose, he could still make the payment. Their business ran on trust. Rashid told Mulliani that he would not allow his reputation as a successful operator to be damaged at any cost.

Mulliani disconnected the call, he was feeling relaxed with the assurance from Rashid. He was about to call Sukhdev but thought otherwise. He came out of the hotel and drove 20 km towards Delhi. On the outskirts of Delhi was Radisson Blu. He parked his car and went inside for breakfast at the ground-level restaurant. During breakfast, he went out and asked the girl standing at the restaurant's entrance, "Can I use this phone?" he pointed towards the phone lying on the counter.

"Do you want to dial outside the hotel?"

"Yes, please."

The girl moved the phone towards him and said,

"Dial zero first."

"Thanks," Mulliani said. He dialed Sukhdev's number. Sukhdev didn't pick up. After waiting for five minutes, he dialled again, and finally, Sukhdev picked up.

"Yes," Sukhdev said.

"Hello, Mulliani, this side."

"What…?" Sukhdev was about to start when Mulliani interrupted and said,

"Please, listen to me carefully. I believe my man travelling to Dubai was apprehended at the airport. I am not sure what exactly has happened. Most probably, they were from the enforcement directorate. I can't talk much on the phone, can you come? We'll talk about it?"

"Where?" Sukhdev asked.

"At Radisson Blu Hotel in Ghaziabad. How much time will you take?"

"It is 8.20 am. I'll try to reach by 9 am."

"Just sit in the lobby and I'll contact you."

Mulliani disconnected the call. The girl at the counter was busy attending to the guests. She did not bother to listen to Mulliani's conversation. He went inside and continued with his breakfast. After 15 minutes, he paid and sat in the lobby. He took out his backup mobile phone, which he turned on the previous night, to call his source at the directorate. His source worked as a peon at the enforcement directorate. He might not have detailed knowledge about the case but would know enough to tell him what had transpired. No one responded. After ten minutes, the peon called back.

"Sir, who is it?"

"Shiv."

"Yes, sir."

"This is Mulliani."

"I've recognized now, sir."

"Where are you?"

"I am outside the building."

"Have they arrested anyone yesterday at night from the airport?"

"I don't know about arrest but I have seen a person sitting in a room. I was asked to bring him breakfast."

"How does he look like?"

Shiv kept describing the person, his height, looks, complexion, the clothes he was wearing, etc. It was now evident that enforcement officials had apprehended Nihal. He said to Shiv,

"Thanks, I may call you again."

"Ok, sir."

It would be dangerous. The cash is three million dollars. Somebody leaked the information. Nihal will be interrogated and follow-up action will be at Nihal's place, Mulliani's shop and residence. His shop and home were clean, and hopefully, Nihal's room will be clean. It all depended on how much they could extract from Nihal during the interrogation.

Mulliani always took care of his employees. If any problem would occur or have occurred, Mulliani considered it his responsibility to hire a lawyer and get his person bailed out. Vikram Pandit was a lawyer with ten years standing in court. Vikram was good and Mulliani had used his services earlier. He called him.

"Hello, who is it?"

"Vikram, this is my number."

"Mulliani?"

"Yes. There seems to be a problem."

"Yes?"

"Yesterday, one of my boys, Nihal Singh, was apprehended at the airport by enforcement officers."

"For carrying currency?"

"Yeah."

"How big is the amount?"

"Three million US dollars."

"Oh hell, Mulliani, you gave them that much money on a platter."

"Yeah, my foolishness, or say my greed."

"Have they arrested him?"

"I am not aware. But he would be arrested. It is certain. You will have to take care of the matter."

"Sure, that's my job. Let me also check what is happening at the ED office. Where are you?"

"On the run, you can say."

"Yeah, stay away for the time being."

"And this is my new number. But avoid calling unless necessary, or I will call. You don't have to worry about your professional charges. You know that."

"Don't worry, sir. Please take care. I'll handle this."

He disconnected the call and while keeping his phone in his pocket, he saw Sukhdev walking in.

* * *

Near the Okala Industrial Area, is a slum across a big vegetable market. Once you cross the vegetable market, you can see a flyover going towards Mathura Road. The well-known hospital, Apollo is situated here. Raghunath had parked his vehicle at the hospital's parking lot and waited. In the morning, there was a lot of rush and the parking lot was almost full. As he switched off his car engine, there was a knock at the other side of the door. Raghunath opened the door and a young boy in his early thirties entered and sat down. He was Raghunath's informer. Raghunath didn't know his real name, but he was known to everyone as Topaz.

"Good morning, sir," Topaz said.

"It was a flop, a big flop. I am in an embarrassing position," Raghunath said.

Topaz said, "Sir, I have again verified. The suitcases must have three million dollars. Also, Mulliani has gone underground. If Mulliani had nothing to do with it, why would he disappear?"

"But, where is the cash? That is what everybody is asking," There was frustration in Raghunath's voice.

"It is strange," Topaz said.

Raghunath said, "If Mulliani, as per your version, had given Nihal the three million in the suitcases, then Nihal has played some mischief." Topaz answered, "Sir, the suitcases were not given to Nihal. These were given to two other boys, who delivered these to Nihal at the departure gate duly placed on a trolley."

That was news for Raghunath. He said, "Then that means Nihal would have to be ruled out."

"Yes, because those two boys, who handed over the suitcases, had proper instructions to watch Nihal and they were not to leave the airport till the flight departed."

That, too was news.

"What about those two boys?" Raghunath enquired.

"That is impossible because they sat in a cab from Mulliani's shop and came directly to the airport. They left the cab."

Raghunath was getting frustrated. He said,

"Then, what happened?"

"Sir, you are the authority. You are to investigate. I can only tell you what I know and I am not lying," Topaz tried to stay calm.

Raghunath kept silent for a while and then asked,

"Can Mulliani help?"

"If you get hold of him?"

"Yes."

"I doubt he is aware of how much has been recovered by the ED. Since he has gone underground, he believes that three million dollars have been nabbed. He would not have bothered for ten thousand dollars. Sir, once he comes to know the details, whosoever has played him, will be dead."

"So, you still stick to your information; it was three million dollars?"

"Yes, sir."

"Do you know who could be the client for whom the money was being transferred?"

"No. That is something, which no one knows."

"Mulliani will be knowing."

Topaz felt that Raghunath was asking too much. He opened the door and said,

"Sir, the information was and is correct. That is all I can say."

He disappeared into the maze of cars in the parking lot. Raghunath looked at his watch. It was already 9:30 am. He texted Samir that he would reach around 10 am.

* * *

"Sir, what happened?" Sukhdev said. He was looking worried. He continued, "You promised the money would be safely transported. My boss has called me thrice since morning and I haven't replied."

Sukhdev's concern was genuine.

Mulliani narrated to him whatever he knew. He further said,

"I have confirmed from my source at the ED right now."

"With our money?" Sukhdev asked.

"Yes, perhaps."

"You mean it's gone?"

"Look, I am working on it, but you'll get the money. I have committed. Trust me, you can assure your boss, they will not lose the money. I have spoken to the people in Dubai. The priority right now is to save ourselves."

"Ourselves?"

"Particularly me. It depends on how much Nihal will tell or has already told them. But I am sure my name would figure. I will have to face the music. Don't worry, your name will not be dragged into this. Once I come out of this, your money will be personally handed over. I will bear all the loss."

"But sir…."

"See, I have told you everything. I am with you. Just bear the delay. Are you sure you have not texted me anything objectionable?" Mulliani asked.

"I have not, but call details will be there," Sukhdev said, adding, "Don't worry about that. I receive 50-60 calls every day. That does not matter."

Quite nervous and confused, Sukhdev got up. Mulliani said,

"My phone is switched off. Don't try to call me. I will remain in touch with you from time to time."

Sukhdev came out of the hotel lobby. He was thinking what he would tell Natasha. He had carried out so many confidential tasks for the company, but this time, when such a big sum of money was involved, he failed. He sat in the car. The time was about 10 am.

* * *

Natasha had reached the office at 9 am, her usual time. She had been through her morning meeting with Archit. Back in her room, she tried to call Sukhdev. He was not responding. She got up and went out of her cabin. Sukhdev's seat was unoccupied.

"Where is Sukhdev?" She asked the employee sitting next to Sukhdev's seat.

"Madam, he is not in yet."

"Ok. Send him in when he comes."

"Sure, madam."

Natasha was back in her cabin. She was wondering what had happened to Sukhdev. Was everything alright? She started getting anxious. She again called Sukhdev. After a few rings, he picked up.

"Hey, where are you? You are not taking my calls."

"Yes, madam, I am on my way but it will take me about two hours to reach there."

"Two hours?"

"Yes, madam. Right now, I have crossed the Ghaziabad-Delhi border."

"What are you doing there?"

"I'll come and explain."

"Is everything all right?"

"Madam I am coming to the office." He disconnected the phone. Natasha realized from his tone that something was wrong and he could not talk on the phone.

"Oh God!" She exclaimed. She leaned back on her chair, closed her eyes, and wondered what bad news Sukhdev would bear.

* * *

Neelesh had no matter listed for hearing. He went through the website looking for judgements passed in the last six months back when Justice Chowdhary was presiding on the bench. He was particularly interested in a judgement where Vinod Goyal had appeared. Finally, he came across the judgement.

In Suman Foundation Vs. Cherry Hills Construction Pvt. Ltd, the PIL was dismissed on frivolous grounds. Suman Foundation was an NGO that worked for environmental causes. Vinod Goyal had appeared on behalf of Cherry Hills Construction Pvt. Ltd., and Suman Foundation was represented by one Vikram Pandit. He had seen Vikram Pandit's nameplate outside one of the cabins in the Delhi High Court. He thought it would not be difficult to find a common acquaintance.

* * * * *

Chapter - X

When Samir returned home, his wife Vidhi was very sleepy. He took the food from the fridge, heated it in the microwave and ate. The following day, Vidhi made the morning tea and woke him up. Samir looked at his watch. It was already 8 am. He looked at his wife and pulled her towards him. Vidhi told him to have the tea and get ready. Samir kissed his wife on the cheek and said,

"Sorry, we missed yesterday's dinner."

"Do you know what was the time when you came back from work?"

"Yes, I know. I can't help that my job is like this. It happens sometimes. I was quite reluctant, but my boss insisted I go with the team."

Vidhi had little idea about the nature of her husband's job. She said,

"At what time do you need to leave today?"

"I have to be at the office by 9:30 am."

Vidhi laughed and said,

"I don't think you will be ready by nine. You are still not done with your bed tea."

"I will try," said Samir, finished his tea and got up. At 9 am he was ready for breakfast. Vidhi said,

"You will need another 15 minutes to finish the breakfast."

His phone beeped. It was the message from Raghunath saying he would be reaching by 10 am. Samir smiled and said to Vidhi,

"My boss is reaching by ten. Now I have sufficient time. Have you started searching for a job?"

Vidhi was a school teacher in Lucknow but left the job to relocate to Delhi after her marriage to Samir. She was searching for a job in different schools. She said,

"Yes, I spent some time yesterday. I have sent requests to two schools. Today, I will follow up."

Samir finished the breakfast and got up. He hugged Vidhi and said,

"Bye. We hope to have dinner together."

"Hope?"

Both laughed.

* * *

At 10:30 am, Raghunath and Samir sat with Ameya in her room. Ameya said,

"So, it turned out to be a flop."

"Yes, madam," Raghunath said.

"Ten thousand dollars only. You have brought the passenger here. What's the name?"

"Nihal Singh."

"Ok, I'll have to appraise the ADG because yesterday night, I indicated to him that there might be a big catch."

Raghunath said,

"Madam, I met the informer in person today. He still sticks to his information that Nihal was given two suitcases containing three million dollars."

"How does that matter? Practically, what we got matters?"

"What I intend to say is Mulliani is reportedly underground now; it means Mulliani is under the impression that we have detained his carrier, Nihal, with three million dollars. Had it been only ten thousand, he would not need to go underground."

Ameya was listening carefully. Raghunath continued,

"As per my information, the suitcases were handed over to two people by Mulliani, who then handed them to Nihal at the airport gate. I am sure that even if we interrogate Nihal, he would not be able to convey much."

"Then…?" asked Ameya.

"Those two boys who brought the suitcases might be able to tell us something," Raghunath suggested.

Samir, who was listening, said,

"Madam, I suggest we seize ten thousand dollars and let Nihal go."

Raghunath said,

"That is the simplest way out, but we know the three million dollars is connected to these people. Shouldn't we try to track that? Even if it is not recovered from Nihal and if we presume that someone embezzled the money, it is for us, to at least attempt to find out where the money went. Only attempt to take out foreign currency is not illegal, but possession of same is also illegal."

Ameya said,

"Ok, Raghunath, I can see that you trust your informer. That is good."

She looked at Samir and said,

"The currency, in any case, has to be seized. First, complete the interrogation and other standard drills of investigation. Perhaps we may get some clue."

Samir asked,

"What about Nihal?"

"We will decide about him later. You have the full day. Use your resources. Let us see if there is any development by evening."

Both Raghunath and Samir came out and sat in Raghunath's room.

"Samir, you start talking to Nihal. Make use of other IOs."

"Right, sir."

"Take the mobile numbers and scrutinize the call details of Mulliani and the two boys who came to the airport. I am sure Mulliani might have switched off the phone. It can help find out the whereabouts of Mulliani. We can send teams to his house and his shop."

"I'll manage, sir," Samir said and left.

Samir decided to make a team of officers to visit Mulliani's shop. He would get the shop's location from Nihal and the residence address would be available at the shop. He kept another team ready to visit Mulliani's house. Samir had a feeling that Mulliani's home would be locked. He took Dinesh, an IO, along with him and went to the room where Nihal was kept through the night.

Nihal was lying on the floor. He had two blankets, as there was a chill in the air. He sat down when both entered. Samir said,

"Nihal, come here," he pointed to a chair placed there. Nihal obeyed. Both Samir and Dinesh sat down before him. Samir said,

"Nihal, do you know why you are here?"

"For those ten thousand dollars."

"Yes. Do you want us to arrest you? You will be sent behind the bars."

"No, sir. I don't want to be arrested."

"Tell us the truth, and we'll allow you to go."

"I've already told the truth."

"No. You have not. Now, you will tell us the truth."

"What is Mulliani's number?"

"It's in my phone."

Samir asked Dinesh to bring Nihal's phone and gave it to Nihal. He said,

"Show me, which one?"

Nihal slid his finger on the screen and said,

"Here it is?"

Samir asked Dinesh to note it down.

"When did you call him last."

"Yesterday. I don't remember the time."

"Had you talked to him when you were at the airport?"

"No."

"You said yesterday that Mulliani handed over both the suitcases to you?"

"Yes, sir."

"True or False?"

"True,"

Samir's tone got harsh."

"Who were the two people who brought the suitcases and handed them over to you? Mulliani never gave you the suitcases. You came to the airport without any suitcases. Right or wrong?"

Nihal kept silent. Samir yelled at him.

"Speak up. True or False. Don't lie, we have the CCTV footage."

"True."

"Who were those two people?"

"They work with me at the shop."

"Names. I am asking the names."

"Prince and Jaydev."

"What are their contact numbers?"

Nihal showed their number on his phone. Dinesh noted down those numbers. He whispered to Dinesh, and Dinesh went away.

"Now tell us whether Mulliani or these two people ever told you the amount of cash in the suitcases."

"No. Never."

"You are lying. It had more money. Where is the rest of it?"

Nihal was confused, but he stuck to his stand,

"Sir, we are never told about the quantum of cash we are to carry. Nor do we ever dare to ask such a thing. Sir, believe me, I am not aware of the quantum. I saw those ten thousand dollars only when you broke open the suitcases."

Samir thought Nihal could be right. Samir got up and went to another room. Dinesh was there. He asked him.

"Anything from the phone number?"

"Mulliani's phone is switched off," Dinesh said.

"What about the other two numbers?"

"These are active. Prince had made two calls to Mulliani yesterday night, probably from the airport. The location will also be confirmed soon. The last call was when Nihal was brought out from the departure. I think they would have seen us escorting him. Mulliani switched off his phone after that."

"Do one thing: put these two numbers on the system. Let us see, Mulliani may call any of them from some other number. He would want to know what's going on."

"Ok."

When Dinesh turned to go, Samir said,

"Also, give Mulliani's number to the officer sitting at the system. He will soon figure out the missing money and might switch on his phone afterwards. We would like to know the details of his client. The client would also be worried, as the cash has not reached Dubai."

"I'll do."

"Once you do this, take two officers to Mulliani's shop. I will get you the address from Nihal."

"Do you think it would be open?" Dinesh asked.

"The shop must be open, but I have doubts about his residence," said Samir and walked towards the room where Nihal was sitting.

* * *

Raghunath looked at the visiting card. It was a lawyer named Vikram Pandit. Raghunath had seen his name in an earlier money laundering or FEMA case. He signaled to the peon and asked him to send the person inside. Vikram Pandit entered and said,

"Good morning, sir."

"Yes, good morning. Please take a seat."

Vikram sat, pulling a chair. Raghunath said,

"Please tell me, how can I help you?"

"Sir, I have a very straightforward query, have your officers detained Nihal Singh from the airport yesterday?"

Raghunath looked at him and wondered how the news had reached the lawyer. He smiled and said,

"What made you think so?"

"Sir, his parents were worried because he had not reached Dubai. Nor is he responding to calls. Then I went to the airline office. They told me that one passenger with this name was offloaded. The reasons were not known to them. Then I went to airport customs, from where I came to know that some officers from ED had come and they might have taken the passenger away."

Raghunath thought Vikram was a professional who knew the trade well. He said,

"Yes, we have detained Nihal Singh."

"Sir, why? Has he done something wrong? I mean, have you recovered anything objectionable?"

"Look, we are investigating."

"Sure, sir. You must be investigating, but have you arrested him or not."

"If and when we arrest him, we will ask him to inform his relatives."

"That means, so far, you have not arrested him. Sir, very politely, can I say that a person cannot be detained longer…"

Raghunath interrupted,

"We know, what we are doing and the law too."

"Sir, who knows the law better than you people! Can I meet him?"

Raghunath started getting irritated. He said,

"I have told you the matter is still under investigation. We are sorry, we cannot permit you to meet him at this stage."

"Sir, please…"

"Mr Vikram, you may go now. If we will arrest him, his parents will be informed. At this stage, I do not know whether his parents authorize you to talk to him.. I think I have given you sufficient time."

Vikram got up, smilingly and said,

"Thank you, sir."

Vikram came out. He expected the conversation to go like this. He had clarity that Nihal was not arrested yet, but the arrest was evident because of the amount of cash involved. The purpose of this visit was to make it clear to the officers that a lawyer had jumped in for Nihal. Now he had to be produced in the court within the stipulated time of 24 hours from when the ED officers took him in for questioning.

* * *

Sukhdev was sitting before Natasha and narrated whatever he learnt from Mulliani. Natasha was sitting dumbfounded. It was a new and scary situation for her. Never in her life had she felt like this. She was on the verge of crying. She wished, she had a sibling or friend with whom she could share the crisis. She blamed herself for getting into this crisis. She controlled herself a bit and said to Sukhdev,

"Can the ED people track down Mulliani?"

"Sooner or later, yes."

"You may also get linked?"

"Mulliani had assured me that my name would not come at any stage."

"Do you believe him?"

"I have no option but to believe him," said Sukhdev.

He was visibly upset. He was the person in direct touch with Mulliani. They both were sitting silently, looking at each other. Finally, she said,

"Sukhdev, you go home right now and try to relax. Don't talk to anyone. Let me see if I can find a way out."

Sukhdev got up. Natasha was looking at him, she said,

"Sukhdev, I am sorry for putting you into this situation."

"Madam, it was the company's job. We both are sailing in the same boat." Sukhdev said and went out. Natasha started crying. She had no one. Finally, she decided to take into confidence Neelesh. Neelesh was a friend and a lawyer, too. He will find a way out. Her main fear was the ED people should not reach her. She could not think of getting arrested. She called Neelesh.

"Neelesh," she said.

"Yeah, what happened, Natasha? Your voice appears as if you…."

Before Neelesh could finish, Natasha broke down on the phone again. After a couple of minutes, she controlled her emotions and said,

"I have to meet you. It is something personal."

"I am at my home. I can come right now."

"Please do come. Just call me when you are outside my office. I will come down."

"Ok, but please don't cry. You are sitting in the office. I am there with you always."

"I am waiting."

She disconnected.

*　*　*　*　*

Chapter - XI

Around 3 pm, Raghunath called Samir and asked for an update on the Nihal Singh case. Samir had interrogated Nihal; however, he hadn't recorded his statement in writing. Samir said,

"Sir, Nihal has nothing further to tell us."

"Or are we not able to extract more?" Raghunath enquired.

"Maybe, sir. Prince called Mulliani twice, and soon after that, Mulliani switched off his phone. Dinesh is at his shop with two officers but nothing suspicious has been recovered on the premises. We have recorded Ravi Chauhan's statement, who is the shop manager at Mulliani's furniture store. In total, there are eight employees, excluding Ravi Chauhan. Seven are present except Nihal. Two officers visited Mulliani's home but it was locked. The mobile numbers of Mulliani, Prince and Jaydev have been added to the system for tracking," Samir said.

"Who are Prince and Jaydev?" Raghunath asked further.

"The two boys who came to the airport handed the suitcases to Nihal. Do you want us to pick up those two for interrogation?" Samir asked.

Raghunath was listening. He said,

"Yes, we can get more information from them, but a development has occurred. Vikram Pandit visited me and was asking about Nihal."

"The lawyer?" Samir asked.

"You know him?"

"I have met him a couple of times in the court. He represented in some of the money laundering and FEMA (Foreign Exchange Management Act) cases. I don't think he is an intelligent lawyer."

"A lawyer needs not to be intelligent. He has to be quick and sharp, which he is."

"What was he saying?"

"He was saying that we should produce him in the court, as per law, within the stipulated time."

"That we will do."

"We have not yet decided whether to arrest him."

"Sir, that is for you to decide."

"I feel that we should arrest him and seek judicial custody."

"The magistrate may give him bail, looking at the amount."

"We have to convince him that there is more to it. The case is being investigated and we cannot allow him to go scot-free."

Samir was not convinced yet. He said,

"Sir, why don't we consult Mr Krishnan, our public prosecutor."

"You are right, Samir. Let's give him the background and the details of the case. He will be able to convince the magistrate."

"Right, sir."

"I will update Ameya madam. You may record his statement and prepare the documents for his arrest."

Samir was smiling. Raghunath looked at him and said,

"What now?"

"Once we apply for Nihal's judicial custody in the court, everyone will know the money recovered is a meagre ten thousand dollars."

Raghunath shrugged his shoulder and said, "We can't help it. Let's call Mr Krishnan to the office and complete all documentation before he arrives."

Samir stood up and went out. At 4:15 pm, Raghunath and Krishnan sat with Ameya in her room. Raghunath narrated the sequence of events starting from receiving the tip and recovering ten thousand dollars. When he finished, Ameya asked,

"What do you think, would it be advisable to arrest Nihal for recovery of ten thousand dollars?" That is around seven lakh INR."

Krishnan picked up the cup of tea lying before him and said slowly,

"No, firstly, you don't arrest for such a small amount. Secondly, even if you decide to do, it is a bailable offence, the magistrate would set him free on furnishing a simple bond."

"We want to arrest him and send him to judicial custody."

Raghunath said, looking at Krishnan,

"Sir, it is not the quantum of seizure alone. Please look at the background. We are trying to bust a big syndicate, as we have information of three million dollars being sent to Dubai."

"But where is the money to substantiate the claim, sir? You have neither been able to recover the cash nor has Nihal confessed anything about the three million dollars. If the seizure of ten thousand dollars is the tip of the iceberg, we need to connect it with three million dollars somehow. There is no evidence to connect these two things at this point."

"Sir, we have the information."

"Information is not evidence."

Ameya was listening. She insisted,

"Mr Krishnan, I want my officers to get an opportunity to investigate."

"Let them do the investigation. Why is the judicial custody so important?"

Raghunath said,

"Sir, the main suspect, the operator Mulliani, thinks that Nihal has been caught with three million dollars. As soon as we produce him in the court, the word will be out the cash recovered was just ten thousand dollars." He paused and looked at both Ameya and Krishnan. Then he added, "Sir I have an intuition that as soon as Nihal is out, he will be dead. So, we feel it is important that Nihal is kept in judicial custody for his safety and we get time to investigate. We are hoping on Mulliani's next move."

Krishnan looked at Ameya and said, "It's difficult. I'll have to speak to the magistrate beforehand."

"Please do," Ameya said.

"When do you intend to produce him?"

"We are ready with documentation; we can produce him right now," Raghunath said.

Krishnan looked at the watch. He said,

"The court normally gets over for the day by 4:30 pm. Let me check."

He called one of his juniors at the court and talked to him for a few minutes. He disconnected and said,

"The court time is over. The magistrate has left."

"Then?" asked Ameya.

"We'll have to produce him at the magistrate's residence. I will talk to him."

He took out his phone and went out. When he came back, he said,

"At the magistrate's residence 6 pm. Ask your officers to arrive a little early. You may ask the accused to talk to his relatives so the lawyer from his side is also there."

Everyone stood up to disperse. Raghunath asked politely,

"Sir, will you be there at his residence?"

Krishnan said, "Yes, and I suggest you should be there too," and left the room.

* * *

Samir asked Raghunath.

"Sir, can I be excused for tonight? I have come to know that you are accompanying the team to the magistrate's place."

Raghunath smiled and said,

"Sure, I'll take care. You can go. Enjoy yourself."

"Thank you, sir."

Samir came out of Raghunath's room. He had not told his boss that he had put Vikram Pandit's number under surveillance. This was done unofficially. The ED officers usually avoided putting any lawyer's number on surveillance. There would be complications if the news leaked. They would go on a strike. The courts would shut down. The department can be slapped with litigation and draw a lot of media ire.

Samir had a gut feeling that Vikram Pandit had come to the ED at the behest of Mulliani. So, as soon as Vikram learnt the cash seized was just ten thousand dollars, he would immediately inform Mulliani. Samir had explicitly asked the officer to listen to the conversation and note Mulliani's new number.

* * *

Krishnan and Raghunath reached Atul Mahajan's house 15 minutes before 6 pm. Atul Mahajan was the Metropolitan Magistrate (MM), residing at Pandara Park. Krishnan briefed the MM about the background of the case. MM smiled and said,

"Krishnan, your department has no case this time. Why do you intend to send an innocent man to jail?"

"Not so innocent and perhaps not at all innocent. The ED wants to gain some time."

There was a knock at the door. Dinesh, the two IOs, along with Nihal came in. MM asked all of them to take their respective seats. Exactly at 6 pm, Vikram entered, holding a *Vakalatnama* duly filled. He bowed before the MM, asked Nihal Singh to sign it and placed it before the MM,

"Lordship, I am representing the accused, Nihal Singh."

"Please take the seat," said MM,

Krishnan moved the application for judicial custody for 14 days. All documents, including *panchnama*, statement of accused, arrest memo, etc., were attached. MM was going through the papers when Vikram said,

"Sir, can I have a set of all these documents, please?"

MM signalled to Krishnan. Dinesh handed over the complete set to Vikram. Vikram looked straight at the Panchnama. His eyes saw the figure of ten thousand US dollars. He was stunned. What was this? Mulliani had told him that it would be three million US dollars. Vikram had prepared the bail application accordingly. Now, he could not produce the same.

"Lordship," Vikram stammered and continued,

"It's only ten thousand US dollars."

MM smiled at him, and said,

"Were you expecting more?"

"No, no, lordship…" Vikram again stammered. He said,

"Why an arrest and application for judicial custody for such a small amount?"

"You can make a bail application and I'll see to it," MM said and extended his hand to take the bail application. That was an embarrassing moment for Vikram. He had made an application but could not produce it. He said,

"My lord, you can grant bail on your own."

"At least you make an application, then I will act upon it. You have not prepared a bail application?" MM Atul Mahajan said.

"Lordship, I'll apply tomorrow morning in the courtroom."

MM smiled. He looked at Krishnan and said, "Today is Tuesday. I am allowing your application. Judicial custody is allowed only for one day. Produce him tomorrow at the regular court and I'll hear both sides." Vikram was about to say something, but MM interrupted and said,

"Mr Vikram, submit your application. I'll consider it on the same day. Without a bail application, I cannot pass any order. Tomorrow, I will take up the matter."

Raghunath was observing Vikram. He thought the informer was correct; neither Mulliani nor Vikram was aware of the amount of cash seized till now. MM, too, looked convinced that Krishnan's briefing was right. Something was fishy.

As MM got up, they all got up. Dinesh and other IO escorted Nihal, who was to be deposited with the police authorities for transportation to prison.

* * *

At 7 pm, when Samir had reached his home, he received a call from the surveillance team that Vikram had called Mulliani, and they were meeting in the lobby of Maurya Hotel at 9 pm. Samir smiled. He called Raghunath.

Samir said, "Sir, Mulliani is meeting Vikram at 9 pm at Maurya."

"How did you manage to know that?"

"Sir, do you want to pick up Mulliani?"

"Sure."

"Then here is the chance."

"But we don't have the officers to accompany us. Dinesh and Ajay are already with the Nihal, handing him over to the prison authorities. You are busy with dinner. Other officers have left."

Samir thought for a moment and said,

"Sir, I can identify Vikram, or you can identify him. I doubt if other IOs will be able to recognize him. We can take four officers from our team and take a few from the system or control room?"

"You will be able to identify him?"

"I will go there with my wife around 8:30 pm. We will be sitting at the Pavilion. I can watch the lobby from there. Let me know the names of the officers coming beforehand. I'll call one of them at the Pavilion and tell them when I see Vikram. Rest is up to them."

"You are smart. Killing two birds with one stone."

Samir smiled and hung up.

*　*　*　*　*

PART - 2

Chapter - XII

A man in his early thirties came out of the Indira Gandhi International Airport's terminal 3 around mid night. He was holding a trolley loaded with two suitcases and stood near gate no.8, the last gate. He looked at his mobile phone, touched the screen and kept moving his fingers. After ten minutes, the Uber cab arrived. The driver helped him place the suitcases in the boot of the cab. The driver asked for the OTP from the man and drove off.

The man sitting in the cab told the driver the cab was for a to-and-fro journey. The destination was Sampla village on the way to Rohtak. It was about a one-and-half-hour journey on one side. The man looked tired. He had not anticipated that coming out of the departure hall without flying would be tedious. He had booked a ticket to Dubai on Air India Express, which was to depart at 11:20 pm IST. A little before 9 pm, he told the airline personnel that due to an emergency, he had to rush back to his home and was not in a position to travel. Initially, no one bothered as all personnel were busy attending to the passengers. Finally, a young girl wearing an Air India uniform took him to an inner cabin. She took his passport and asked about his baggage. His name was Pratap Singh. Then she told Pratap that he would have to wait until the flight departed. Once the flight left, she made some entries in her system and took him along with his baggage to the airport security office. The officer sitting there asked a few questions to Pratap and gave the written permission for Pratap to exit. The Air-India personnel escorted Pratap and his baggage to the security personnel operating the exit gate. The girl left him outside exit gate no. 8. This was the end of a two-hour-long ordeal for Pratap.

Pratap was a close friend of Nihal and both belonged to Sampla village. Nihal had told Pratap that there was an opportunity to make big money for both of them. Nihal bought two new suitcases and handed them over to Pratap, fully packed and locked. Nihal had asked one of the travel agents to arrange a visa for Pratap urgently. The travel agent told him it would be difficult to get it on such a short notice. It was not required as Pratap was not going to travel. The visa was never checked at the entry gate. Nihal told them that if anyone asked for it, he should say he intended to get it on arrival in Dubai.

The plan for Pratap was to enter the departure hall with those two suitcases and wait for Nihal. On seeing Nihal, Pratap would leave his trolley outside the washroom, and when Pratap came out of the washroom, Nihal would leave his trolley outside the washroom, and enter. Pratap would swap his trolley with Nihal's. Once it was done, Nihal would board the flight and Pratap would come out of the departure hall by telling the airline staff that he could not continue his travel due to some emergency at home, and needed to rush back.

Everything happened as planned, and Pratap was out with two suitcases full of cash. Nihal was, however, yet to tell Pratap the exact amount of cash in the suitcases.

Pratap's father had installed a stone crusher on a piece of land on the outskirts of Sampalavillage. While coming from Delhi, it was little before the village. It was visible from the highway. When Pratap's father passed away four years back, Pratap moved to Delhi. The glamour and dazzling lights of the big city attracted him. The crusher was lying idle and had turned into junk. The land was covered by a brick boundary wall, with a gap for truck and dumper entry. Near this entry was a small room meant for the security guard, when the crusher was in working condition. The room was Pratap's current destination. It was a perfect hideout. He would leave those two suitcases for a few days until Nihal returned from Dubai.

Finally, the cab reached the destination. The driver helped Pratap in taking out the suitcases. Pratap brought both suitcases into the room. It was dark and when Pratap threw some light, he could see a cot on the concrete floor. He placed both the suitcases under the cot and covered those with an old and dusty bed sheet. He came out, locked the room properly and sat in the cab. He told the driver,

"Let us go back to Delhi."

Nihal and Pratap had decided not to text or call each other.

* * *

Natasha sat with Neelesh in his car and asked Kishan to take them to her Gurugram home. Neelesh wanted to talk to her, but she was gloomy and preferred to remain quiet as Kishan, the driver, was also in the car. She had instructed Kuku beforehand to reach Gurugram.

Once they were inside her apartment, Natasha started crying. Neelesh hugged her to console her.

"What's the matter? Please tell me. I am getting worried."

It took her some time to control herself. She sipped some water and cuddled in Neelesh's arm. Then, she started narrating the events from the day she discovered the cash in US dollars from her father's box bed and how she learnt the courier sent by Mulliani had been apprehended. Neelesh was listening carefully. When she finished, Neelesh said,

"Why didn't you tell me earlier? We could have found a solution."

"Put yourself in my place; my father had an impeccable reputation. He was an upright man. It came as a shock when I discovered the cash. I couldn't believe it. Telling someone, even you, would mean putting a question mark on his reputation. That was something I never wanted, particularly when he was no more. One cannot tarnish the image of a person when he is no longer there. It took me many days to reconcile with the situation."

"I can understand but you could have taken me in confidence."

"My concern is not that the money is gone. I am concerned is the ED officials might find a link to me."

She started crying again and said, "Neelesh, I don't want to go to prison. I am so scared."

Neelesh pulled her closer in her arms and said,

"Natasha, you are not alone in this. We are in it together. We will try to find a way out. Natasha kept crying. Neelesh thought the judgement in the case of Cherry Hills Construction Pvt. Ltd., the last judgement by Natasha's father, was connected to this money.

Natasha was looking at him. She said, "I have heard the ED is a very elite agency and they have resources to track the money."

"Yeah, to some extent. Tell me, how trustworthy is Sukhdev? You have never met or called Mulliani, right? The only connection is Sukhdev. I am sure ED may reach up to Sukhdev. Sukhdev has to be strong."

"He is trustworthy."

"Natasha, you don't know. If push comes to shove, will he not try to save himself? The person you consider most trustworthy can be the one who deceives you," Neelesh responded.

"You are a lawyer. Your clients must have faced such a situation. How do you deal with such a situation?"

Neelesh was thinking about the three million dollars. He was aware the whole system works on trust in the underworld. There is nothing on record. Mulliani would not have tried to pocket the money. However, foul play by one of his employees cannot be ruled out and the doubt goes on the person carrying the suitcases. He said,

"Let me see. Tomorrow, I will find out from the court who is handling the matter and what is the real position. You keep calm."

Neelesh got up to leave. He wanted to make a sequence of events. He patted Natasha and said,

"I will go now and call you tomorrow. Meanwhile, don't discuss it with anyone, even informally, either in person or over the phone."

Natasha nodded; she had a strange feeling about Neelesh. He didn't want to stay with her when she needed the most. She called Kishan and asked him to go, leaving the keys. When Kishan left, she sat down and cursed herself.

* * *

Vidhi and Samir were sitting in the Pavilion. Samir intentionally selected a table from where he could have a clear view of the lobby. The time was 8:30 pm. Vidhi looked at him and said,

"Hey, are you ok?"

"Yes, why?" asked Samir.

"You don't seem to be interested in me. You are not even looking at me."

"Vidhi, there is a small job. It is official. I am not participating. But two suspects are meeting here in the lobby at 9 pm. I am to identity them."

Vidhi said tauntingly,

"So, this dinner is just a pretence?"

"No dear," Samir held her hand. He continued, "I am telling you my job is just to identify the person. My other colleagues will be here. After nine or maybe even before that, I am all yours."

Vidhi kept quiet. Lunch and dinner at the Pavilion are usually buffet meals. He asked Vidhi,

"Will you prefer a buffet, or shall we order a la carte?"

She shrugged and said,

"I don't know, what all they have in the buffet?"

"You can go and have a look."

Vidhi got up. Samir saw a person in his late forties or early fifties entering the lobby. He looked around and sat on a corner sofa. Samir presumed that this person could be Mulliani. There was a beep on his phone. It was Deven, one of the IOs from his office. Samir called him to come inside the Pavilion and waved to him. Samir said,

"Deven, is a person sitting alone? He seems to be waiting for someone. How many IOs are there?"

"Four, in total."

"Look, I can identify Vikram when he comes in the lobby and goes to someone. Then that someone has to be Mulliani. What I want is, if possible, you pick up Mulliani before Vikram starts talking. Thus far; Vikram has not told him about the total amount of cash seized."

"Sir, who told you?" asked Deven.

Samir smiled and said,

"The officer at the system." He continued,

"Ok, now go. Be near that man sitting in the corner. I will message 'yes' if he is the person. Keep your phone handy."

"But, sir, it is a public place. If he resists."

"Don't worry about that. Just pick him up and take him to the office. Be in touch with Raghunath sir."

Deven went out. Vidhi came and said,

"They have a lot of items. How can one eat so much?"

"We are not to eat all items, Vidhi."

"I know that much. But you have a look. It is a grand buffet."

Samir saw Vikram entering the lobby and approached the man sitting in the corner. The man stood up to greet Vikram. Samir immediately sent the message and saw Deven and others covering the man. He didn't resist. Vikram was standing, not knowing what to do. Samir got up and asked Vidhi,

"Come, let us have the dinner."

"Your job is over?"

"Yes."

* * *

Nihal was sent to the prison. He thought that everything went as planned except for his arrest. This was not anticipated. Nihal had been working with Mulliani for the last six years. He had taken trips to Singapore, Hong Kong and Dubai several times. He used to carry cash in his handbags. Sometimes, he was told that there was cash in the bag. At other instances, he was not told but he presumed that Mulliani had used him for the same purpose. He was being paid Rs 25,000 monthly and had seen a lot of money coming and going. In Hawala transactions, cartons full of Indian Rupees were used to be delivered. Along with Prince and Jaydev, he would count it and deliver it to local persons, as and when Mulliani would say.

Of late, he was thinking about starting his own business in Hawala. He had learnt all the tricks, secrets and methods. This idea was gradually taking shape in his mind. When he was told to carry an amount of three million US dollars, on Sunday, it struck to his mind that it was the right time. He knew that Mulliani would not spare him, but then he thought an opportunity like this would never come again.

Nihal and Pratap belonged to the same village. They were close to each other. He told Pratap about his plan. He, however, did not tell him the quantum of money and that it would be in US dollars. He told Pratap that a huge amount would to be transported by him. But then he could not handover empty suitcases to Rashid at Dubai. He borrowed about seven lakhs from a money lender on interest and promised to return it within a month. He intended to place ten thousand dollars in the suitcases so that when Rashid finally opened the suitcases, at least some money would be there, so Nihal could say that whatever was given to him had been handed over. He intended to stay back in Dubai for a while. The two new suitcases were bought, and a ticket for Pratap was arranged. All went well, but the ED officers intercepted him. As he kept thinking, a new idea clicked. He smiled.

* * * * *

Chapter - XIII

It was easy for Neelesh to find out who appeared before the MM. However, he did not know the name of the accused. The next day, he went to the district court. Had there been a case with the recovery of three million US dollars, it would be the talk of the town. He sat in the bar room. Nobody was talking about any such suit. He could not make out anything from the cause list. He saw Krishnan's junior entering the bar room. Krishnan was a senior lawyer respected by all. Neelesh knew that Krishnan was on the panel of the ED as a Public Prosecutor. He called out to his junior Avdesh.

Neelesh said, "Hey, Avdesh."

"Good morning, sir," Avdesh responded.

"How is Mr Krishnan?"

"He is good."

"Is he in the chamber?"

"No, but he will be here during the post-lunch sessions."

"Any matter listed for him?"

"The ED produced an accused yesterday at MM's residence. MM gave one day's custody and directed that he be produced today."

"It must be a big matter," Neelesh said.

"Oh, no. Not at all. Just recovery of ten thousand dollars."

"Do they arrested for such a small amount?"

"Normally, they don't," Avdesh said and shrugged his shoulders.

"Who is the accused?"

"Nihal Singh."

Neelesh looked at him and smiled. Avdesh got up and started talking to other fellow lawyers sitting there. Neelesh didn't want to directly ask him about the case of three million US dollars.

* * *

Samir and Dinesh entered the room where Mulliani was sitting. Both these officers were not there the previous night when Mulliani was apprehended. When the officials walked up to him, Mulliani asked,

"What is all this, sir? Why have I been detained here all night?"

Both pulled their respective chairs and sat down.

"Yes, we are about to figure that out, Mr Mulliani?" Samir said.

He continued, "Do you know Nihal Singh?"

"Yes, he is one of my employees," Mulliani replied.

"Some foreign currency has been recovered from him in the baggage and as per his statement, the baggage was handed over to him by you."

"But that's wrong."

"Why would Nihal take your name?"

"Sir, I handed over the suitcases to two of my other employees, who might have handed over those to Nihal."

"On that. Yes, you corrected us. That is exactly what he stated to us."

Dinesh asked Mulliani,

"How much cash in US dollars was there in the suitcases?"

"Sir, you have opened and checked it," Mulliani responded.

"Yes, it is in our knowledge. We are cross-checking," Dinesh said.

"Ten thousand," Mulliani said.

Samir and Dinesh were taken aback. Samir had tried his best that Mulliani was to be apprehended before Vikram could talk to Mulliani. But Mulliani knew the number. Samir said,

"Did Vikram tell you?"

"Sir, as you say, those bags were given by me. I must be aware of the amount, placed in those suitcases. No third person needs to tell me?"

Their complete line of questioning got scattered. They were expecting Mulliani, to say three million US dollars. There was a lapse. Samir thought for a moment and asked Dinesh,

"Where is his mobile phone?"

"Must be with Deven," Dinesh replied.

"Go, bring it," a frustrated Samir said.

In the next five minutes, Mulliani's phone was with them. Samir checked the call details. There was a call the previous day from Vikram. He checked the messages. he message box was empty.

"Have you deleted the messages?"

"No, sir."

Mulliani knew the ED officers had nothing much to ask. Vikram's junior had sent him a message yesterday which read,

"It is not three million. The amount recovered from Nihal was ten thousand US dollars."

Mulliani had got the biggest shock as it was impossible. He had complete faith in Nihal, Prince and Jaydev. He thought for a moment that time and deleted the message. It was smart on Vikram's end not to use his phone. They heard Mulliani saying,

"Sir, may I go? I have not slept the whole night. I admit that I gave ten thousand dollars. I import furniture, and sometimes, the amount in the invoice is shown on the lower side. This was the balance over and above the invoice amount, which was to be remitted to the supplier. I know it may not be legal, but as the amount was not much, I took the chance."

Samir said,

"You seem to have been well tutored."

"Sir, may I go?"

"Be seated. We'll tell you when you can leave."

"Please, sir."

Samir and Dinesh came out and looked at each other. They went to Raghunath's room and told him about their conversation with Mulliani. Raghunath said,

"So, it turned out to be a futile exercise."

"It so seems," Samir said.

"Sir, Mulliani insists that he should be allowed to go," Dinesh said.

"That's natural. He knows, you have nothing against him. He knows you cannot arrest him. Even Nihal's arrest was not warranted. MM will hear the matter today. Dinesh, you should go to the court."

"Yes, sir."

"I contacted Mr Krishnan's office. The matter will be taken up at 2:30 pm." Dinesh said.

Raghunath looked at the watch and said,

"You must leave, then."

"Sir, what shall we do with Mulliani?"

"Record his statement, whatever he is saying and allow him to go. We have no option."

Both Samir and Dinesh came out. Raghunath picked up the phone and briefed Ameya on the latest developments.

* * *

At 2:30 pm, Nihal was brought into the court under police escort. Vikram was sitting in the front row. He got up and went near Nihal. He told him that there was nothing to worry about and that Nihal would get the bail. Nihal just smiled. Atul Mahajan was hearing some other matter. The courtroom was crowded with lawyers. Mr Krishnan, with one of his juniors entered. In another five minutes, the MM called for Nihal Singh's case. The court master placed the file before the MM. He glanced through the file and looked at Krishnan.

"Yes, Mr Krishnan. It's a small matter. Why do you want 14-days custody?"

Krishnan came forward and said,

"Lordship, the recovered amount is ten thousand dollars and the arrest has not been made simply on the ground of this recovery. The department is investigating the matter. The case has larger ramifications. The department has intel that a complete syndicate is working; this recovery is just the tip of the iceberg. The department is continuing the investigation and needs time to interrogate the accused, Nihal Singh thoroughly. The department is working on other leads also."

Atul Mahajan was listening. These were routine pleadings from the prosecutors. He looked at Nihal Singh and then at Vikram Chauhan and said,

"Have you made the bail application?"

"Yes, Lordship."

"You want to bail immediately?"

"Yes, lordship."

"Say what you have to say." Atul Mahajan looked at the bail application and continued.

"You didn't make an application yesterday. It is here now with me."

Krishnan interrupted,

"Lordship, there is no case of immediate bail. It is a case..."

Atul Mahajan smiled at Krishnan and said, looking towards Vikram.

"Let him justify his presence."

As Vikram was about to start, Nihal raised his hand and said,

"Sir, I have something to say."

Vikram sharply looked at him and signalled him to be quiet. Nihal again said,

"Sir, I have something important to tell the court if permitted."

There was a pin-drop silence. Everyone looked at Nihal. Atul Mahajan looked at Vikram smilingly and questioningly. He finally said,

"Yes, Mr Nihal Singh. We will first hear you."

Nihal came a step forward, folded his hands and started speaking,

"Sir, I was travelling to Dubai and when I reported at the airline counter. A few officers took me away to a separate room along with my suitcases. There were six or seven people, and I learnt later that they were officers from the ED. They asked me to unlock the suitcases, I was unaware of the combination lock so they broke it. There were three million US dollars in those suitcases. They counted it there and put all the cash back in suitcases. I was made to sit in a car with them and brought to the ED office. I have not seen those suitcases after that. They prepared some documents and I was asked to sign those. I asked them what was in those papers. They told me these were documents about the US dollars from my baggage. I signed those documents under the belief that they mentioned three million dollars. Yesterday, when I was brought to your home, I heard this man, he pointed towards Vikram and continued, saying that it's only ten thousand US dollars. Sir, I could not understand, at that time, what was happening and what amount he was referring to. I was also not allowed to tell the exact amount in the suitcases."

Everybody in the courtroom was listening to something which they had never heard. Krishnan looked at Dinesh and got up to protest. Ajay Mahajan signalled to him and said,

"Let him finish."

Vikram was stunned. He did not expect this turn of events. Nihal said,

He pointed towards Krishnan and said, "Sir, now when I thought and listened to him, it occurred to me that when there were three million dollars in those suitcases, why is everyone talking about ten thousand dollars? I must bring it in the knowledge of the court."

Vikram was about to say something. Ajay Mahajan silenced him and asked Nihal.

"You mean to say that when the officers opened the suitcases, there were three million dollars."

"Yes, sir."

"Do you realize that you are implicating yourself in a major offence?"

"Sir, I do not know about the major or minor, I am simply narrating the facts."

"When the suitcases were opened or broken, who was in that room?"

"Those six, seven officers."

"Anybody else?"

"One officer was in white uniform, maybe from customs."

"No one else?"

"No, sir."

Ajay Mahajan picked up the *panchnama* from the side and looked at Nihal's signature. He asked,

"Are these your signature?"

"Yes, sir."

"You signed these documents at the airport, in that room?"

"No, sir. As I told you, I was brought to the ED office and my signatures were taken there.

Vikram thought Nihal had turned the tables on the ED, but he was unsure how the MM would take it, but he made up his mind about what he had to say. Krishnan was thinking that Nihal is in fact, directly implicating the ED officers in the embezzlement of the cash during recovery. Ajay Mahajan looked at Krishnan and said,

"Yes, Mr Prosecutor. Can you throw some light on what the accused is saying?"

Krishnan was an experienced lawyer. He had seen many embarrassing positions during court proceedings, but he always knew how to wriggle out. He said,

"Lordship, there is a *panchnama*. The recovery has been made in the presence of two independent witnesses. He has been tutored just to defame my client, the ED office. The *panchnama* was drawn at the airport."

Ajay Mahajan could sense the direction of proceedings. This meant the officers had pocketed all the money. Though it was an allegation by an accused, such an allegation could not be ignored. It was going to become a big news. He looked at the courtroom. There were more than 40 lawyers. After a moment's thought, he told Krishnan and Vikram to meet him in his chamber. Ajay Mahajan got up and went in from the door at the back. Both Krishnan and Vikram followed him.

Once, in Ajay Mahajan's chamber, Ajay yelled at Krishnan.

"What the hell is all this?"

"Lordship Nihal is lying."

"I have not called you here to hear all this. Vikram, did you tutor him to speak all this?"

"Lordship, I had no opportunity to meet him. He was supposed to be carrying three million dollars. The person who asked me to represent him told me that Nihal had been apprehended with three million dollars. Yesterday, when we were at your residence, I had prepared the bail application on the presumption that he was carrying three million dollars, but when I saw the papers, I was shocked. I could not have produced that application before your Lordship. No lawyer will appear without a bail application if he is to seek bail."

Vikram opened his folder and took out a bunch of folded - paper. He said,

"Lordship, I still have yesterday's application. You can see it was prepared with the presumption the recovery amount would be three million dollars."

Ajay Mahajan glanced through the papers and tossed them towards Krishnan, who looked at them. Ajay Mahajan looked into the eyes of Krishnan and said slowly as if whispering.

"You too briefed me on the same lines yesterday."

"Lordship, he has given a statement admitting recovery of ten thousand dollars," Krishnan said.

"Don't tell me all that, I know how statements are taken."

"But, Lordship, he is telling a lie. The ED officials can never do such a thing."

"I know they can't do it, but prove it. Recover the amount or evidence. Go to the courtroom; I am coming."

In another 15 minutes, the court resumes its work. Ajay Mahajan asked the stenographer to take the dictation.

"The accused, Nihal Singh, has made a serious allegation against officers of the ED. In the absence of evidence regarding three million

US dollars, there appears to be no substance in the accused's allegation. But looking at the gravity of the allegation, this court cannot overlook the same. I hereby order the Director General of ED or any other officer superior to thoroughly investigate the matter. The result of such an investigation has to be submitted to this court within 15 days.

Regarding the recovery of ten thousand US dollars from the accused, the ED is at liberty to continue their investigation. However, looking at all the circumstances, the court has observed that there is prima facie no case of prosecution, and hence, the bail is granted to the accused with immediate effect."

Ajay Mahajan concluded the order and talked to the court master for a few minutes. He said,

"The court is adjourned for today. Any further matters listed for today will be taken up later on. The next date of hearing would be conveyed."

Ajay Mahajan got up and returned to his chamber without looking at anyone.

Neelesh was sitting in the last row and had watched all the case proceedings.

* * * * *

Chapter XIV

As soon as Vikram came out of the courtroom, he first needed to appraise Mulliani, but he could not contact him because the ED officers had picked him up the night before. Mulliani would not have the phone on him at the moment. He thought he should go to the ED office. However, he decided to call him. After 8-10 rings, Mulliani picked up,

"Yes, Vikram."

"Where are you?" At the ED office?

"I have just come out. They have released me."

"Had your statement been recorded?"

"Yes," said Mulliani surprisingly.

"Had they asked about the money in the suitcases?"

"Yes, what happened? Why are you asking so many questions and that too on the telephone."

"Nihal Singh created havoc in the court. He told the magistrate when the ED officers opened the suitcases at the airport, it had three million dollars, but the recovery of only ten thousand dollars was shown."

"What? That fool. Did he say that in court?"

"Yes. The magistrate called the public prosecutor (PP) and me to his chamber. He was quite annoyed. Nihal's statement in the court is a direct allegation that officers of the Enforcement Directorate have embezzled money. What have you written in your statement?"

"Ten thousand US dollars. Where is he?

"Who? Nihal?"

"Yes, yes."

"He got bail, and the magistrate has ordered a detailed enquiry. Do you understand all this? It is enmity with the department.

"Where is he?"

"I told you; Nihal has been given bail."

"Is he with you?"

"No, he will be in police lock-up at court only. Once the police will receive the court order in writing, he will be released."

"Vikram, I need to talk to him. I am coming to the court premises. Please ensure Nihal stays with you till I come."

"I will try."

"What do you mean try? Go to the court, take the order and don't produce the order before police authorities till I come."

"Ok."

Vikram disconnected the call and went to the courtroom. It was empty. He went to the office where the court staff's workstations were. He walked up to Ajay Mahajan's stenographer and said,

"Madam, has Nihal Singh's bail order been signed?"

She smiled and said,

"Yes, sir."

"Can I, have it? I am the one who was representing him."

"Sir, it has been handed over to police authorities. If you need a copy, I can get one."

Vikram rushed out and went towards the prisoner's lockup. It was on the left side of the court compound. He moved briskly. Near the entrance, he was stopped by a guard.

"Sir, may I help you?"

"I am to take release of a prisoner."

"Sir, you may go to the second room on the right side of the corridor. The officers sitting there have all the details.

Vikram went out to that room and enquired about Nihal Singh. He was told that Nihal was released about five minutes ago. He came out and looked around. There were a few small eateries around that place. He looked there. Nihal was not to be seen anywhere. He called Mulliani,

"Sir, Nihal has been released five minutes ago. The bail order was served before I could reach."

Mulliani kept silent. He was a seasoned player of the game. He knew Nihal's outburst in the court had a reason behind it. Nihal would have never stated like that. Either as he claimed the ED officers had intentionally misappropriated or he was double-crossing Mulliani. As far as Mulliani knew, a team of ED officers would not embezzle money like this. Bribes and hefty bribes were heard of, but if a case was filed, it was made perfectly. If it had happened, this might have been an isolated incident. The second probability could be that Nihal had other plans with the money, and now, to justify his act, he was blaming the

ED. Mulliani could not believe the first possibility and his experience was telling him that Nihal was trying to take advantage of the situation. If that was the case, Mulliani had no answer to the question 'How'?

He called Prince,

"Hello,"

"Yes, sir,"

"Do you know where Nihal lives?"

"Yes, sir. I have been to his house."

"Look, Nihal has been released on bail. He might or might not go to his home. You go to his house. Take Jaydev with you and see if he is there. If he is there, stay with him and call me to update."

"Right, sir."

"Leave right now," Mulliani instructed before disconnecting.

* * *

Neelesh had watched the entire drama unfold in the courtroom during Nihal's hearing. He knew that whatever Nihal had said was without Vikram knowing about it. He could see that written on Vikram's face. Natasha had told Neelesh the amount of three million US dollars. Nihal was correct to that extent. All persons of his fraternity firmly believed that agencies like the Enforcement Directorate never indulge in embezzlement. From Nihal's statement, it appeared that Nihal was at least aware of three million dollars in those suitcases. He called Natasha,

"Natasha,"

"Yes," she replied as if she was sleepy.

"Are you not at the office?"

"I took the day off. I could not sleep last night. I had to take a pill early in the morning."

"Sleeping pill?"

"Yeah. What's it? Have you any news?"

"Yes, I was in the courtroom at the time of Nihal's hearing. There was some interesting development. I'll come and explain."

"I am at home."

"Coming in an hour."

* * *

When Vikram entered his chamber, he got a surprise. Nihal was sitting there. Vikram exclaimed,

"How come are you here?"

"They released me. I asked someone about your chamber and came here."

Vikram took his phone to inform Mulliani. Nihal said,

"Are you calling Mulliani?"

"Yes. I was looking for you. I went to the prisoner's lock up, and they said you were released. Mulliani wanted to see you. I will tell him, and he will be here in another half an hour. We will have tea by that time."

Nihal looked at him and said,

"Don't call Mulliani. I have come to you for a purpose. First, listen to me and then you can decide whether to call him or not."

Vikram kept the phone on his table and asked the office boy to bring two cups of tea. He looked at Nihal and said,

"Yes, tell me."

"I want my passport. It is with the ED. You can get it from them now as I am released on bail."

"What's the hurry?"

"You see, in all probability, they'll give the passport because the ED is under pressure right now. My bail is unconditional. Tomorrow, they might create several reasons to avoid releasing the passport. They had my mobile phone and taken one hundred dollars from me. It is on record."

Vikram smiled at him and said,

"Whatever you said at court, was that a truth?"

"You see, I was to get the bail even otherwise. I had heard the ED officers talking, as it was a small case."

"Was that all truth?"

"Mr Vikram, you get my passport today and I'll pay you your fee. You are representing me."

"No. I am representing Mulliani, you know that. Mulliani is paying my professional charges."

"Sir, I'll pay you double what Mulliani will pay."

The office boy had served the tea and left. It was evident to Vikram that Nihal had all the money. Once he would have the passport, he would leave the country. He smiled and said,

"You have still not answered my question."

"Sir, one is required to speak the truth in court."

"So, you have learned things."

"Can you help me in getting my passport? Or, I'll go myself and get it; I am not scared of visiting the ED office. At least not today."

"I'll charge four times. Two times my professional charges, which you have promised and rest for not telling Mulliani that you had come to me."

"How much is he paying?"

Vikram laughed and said,

"Come with me in my car. We'll go to the ED office. You need not come in, just keep sitting in the car."

Nihal got up but was suspicious. He said,

"And while I sit in your car, Mulliani and his boys would approach me."

Vikram said,

"You can trust me or you cannot, but those are your only options."

They both sat in the car and went away.

* * *

The nameplate outside the room read, "Rajan Mathur, Director General." A red light outside the room was flashing, indicating that he was in a meeting and that no one was allowed to go in.

Krishnan, Ameya, Raghunath and Samir sat before a long semi-circular table. On the other side was Rajan Mathur. Ameya had summoned Krishnan also when she was told about the developments in the court that day. The time was 5.20 pm. Rajan was agitated to say the least. He asked Ameya about the case. She narrated the complete sequence of events, starting from the tip to what subsequently happened. Ranjan turned to Krishnan and said,

"What exactly has the court ordered?"

Krishnan said, "Sir, the court said that there was no substance in whatever the accused had alleged, but looking at the gravity of the allegation, the same could not be overlooked. The court ordered that an officer at least of the level of DG should conduct an enquiry and the report has to be submitted to the court within 15 days."

"Mr Krishnan, you are a senior lawyer. Don't you think such observations of the court or the order of the court could have been avoided? You know how embarrassing it is? It will be in the media tomorrow or maybe in electronic media tonight. They keep looking for such scandals.

Raghunath and Samir were listening. Krishnan said,

"Sir, the magistrate got prejudiced. When Ameya madam briefed me, the tip was for three million dollars, I had to take the magistrate into confidence beforehand. On that briefing only, he agreed for judicial custody. The next day, the opposition lawyer produced a bail application he had drafted earlier that mentioned the amount of three million dollars. The accused, Nihal Singh, quoted the amount as three million dollars. All these events coincided and the magistrate got prejudiced that something was fishy which was not being brought on record."

Rajan looked at Ameya,

"What will we do about the media?"

Ameya kept mum. She was cursing why she permitted Raghunath to go ahead with the information. Raghunath said,

"Sir, whatever Nihal had stated in court is all lies."

"I know that, you know that, everybody knows that, but…"

There was a ring on Rajan's landline. He pressed the button and spoke in angry tone.

"I told you not to give me any call."

"Sir, it is from the Ministry." It was her secretary. He immediately picked up the receiver and kept listening. The call lasted not more than one minute. He slammed down the receiver and said,

"The ministry has asked me to meet at 9:30 am tomorrow. The news has travelled.

Krishnan said,

"Sir, the lies diffuse farther, faster, deeper and more broadly than the truth."

Rajan looked at Krishnan and said sarcastically,

"Good quotation at the wrong time."

Rajan signalled all to get up. The meeting was over. Krishnan, however, stayed back.

Ameya, Raghunath and Samir came out and saw Dinesh waiting outside. Ameya stopped and said,

"What now?"

"Nihal's lawyer has been here for half an hour requesting to release his passport."

Before Raghunath or Samir could speak something, Ameya said sharply.

"Release it."

And she briskly walked away.

* * *

Natasha had just sprinkled water on her face. The whole day, she was feeling drowsy. She prepared a coffee and settled down on her couch as she waited for Neelesh. He arrived at about 6:30 pm. She opened the door with a coffee mug in her hand. With one arm, she hugged him. Neelesh stepped in and closed the door behind him.

"So, you took the day off today?"

"Couldn't sleep the whole night."

"Take it easy."

"What happened?"

"I was in the court. Nihal Singh is the name of the person who was carrying the money. And …"

"And what?" asked Natasha.

Neelesh wanted to tell her the story narrated by Nihal but then recollected that Natasha was unaware of the amount of money recovered. He initially intended not to tell her, but then it suddenly occurred to him that it would be in the media by tomorrow. "And there were a lot of arguments from both sides. Nihal Singh said the suitcases had three million dollars, and the officers stated it had ten thousand dollars."

"It doesn't make sense. I placed three million dollars in suitcases."

"So, in this dispute, the magistrate got annoyed, and ordered further investigation."

Neelesh could have told her that it was a case of ten thousand dollars and Nihal got a bail, but he refrained.

"What do you mean by further investigation?"

"To enlarge the area of investigation."

Natasha got scared.

"So, they can question me?"

"Don't worry. I told you the other day. You are not in the picture. It was only Sukhdev, who met Mulliani and not you."

Natasha was uncomfortable. While, Neelesh was planning on his own to find out where the money was hidden. He consoled Natasha.

"I am with you. I am taking care of all the things. Your problems are my problems."

"Would you stay with me here tonight?" asked Natasha.

Neelesh smiled and said,

"Yes, if you wish so. You need not take a sleeping pill tonight."

* * *

Nihal was sitting in the car outside the ED's office. Even though he anticipated Vikram to call Mulliani and rat him out, but he had no option. He couldn't go to his home. He was sure Mulliani must have sent someone to look for him. He had an urge to contact Pratap. He wanted to ensure that all was well at Pratap's end and the money right now.

He saw Vikram coming towards the car. He opened the door and sat at the driving seat. He smiled at Nihal and said,

"Here is your passport, mobile phone and a hundred dollar note. That was what you wanted."

"Thank you, sir. It is a big obligation."

"Forget the obligation. When are you paying my fee."

"Sir, just give me two days. I promise. Right now, my pockets are empty."

"And if you leave the country before that?"

"Sir, I'll not leave the country unless I pay you. And please can you keep these 100 dollars and give me some Indian currency. I need it."

Vikram laughed and handed him Rs. 5,000. He said,

"This is what I have right now. Keep that note with you. And tell me where to drop you."

"Ok, sir."

* * *

Nihal lived in a rented one-room apartment in Inderpuri. Prince and Jaydev found that his house was locked. The building had three floors. When one climbed the stairs, there were two flats on each floor. The apartment on the left side was unoccupied. Both Prince and Jaydev looked around. It appeared the house was locked for quite some time. Prince called Mulliani and told him. Mulliani said,

"Is there a way to enter?"

"No, sir. The lock has to be opened. That is the only entry," Prince replied.

"Can you open the lock?"

"I can try."

"Try, if it is possible. We don't want to alarm the neighbours."

"There appears to be no one residing in the opposite flat to his."

"Wait till 11 pm. He may possibly come."

"Ok."

* * *

Nihal took an autorickshaw and went to a shopping mall in Rajouri Garden. Pratap worked a job in a shop there. His shift was till 8 pm.

There were no customers in the shop at that time. Pratap saw him coming and quickly came out and met Nihal. Nihal asked,

"Hey, is the money safe?"

"Yes," said Pratap and smiled.

"Look, I was arrested at the airport, but now I am out on bail. Mulliani must be on the lookout for me. I can't go to my flat."

Pratap patted on Nihal's shoulder and said, "Stay with me."

"You give me the keys to your house. I'll go. Take some rest till you come."

Pratap took out the keys and handed them to Nihal.

At 8:30 pm, Pratap joined him. Nihal narrated the events since they parted in the airport to Pratap. Nihal said,

"Pratap, we have to arrange for some money. I have to pay to Vikram and I have to pay to the money lender from whom the money was borrowed."

"How much money do you need in total?"

"Around seven lakhs to the money lender and one lakh to Vikram. I don't know. Vikram may demand more."

"We can take out some money from the suitcases that we have hidden."

"Yes. But we have to be careful. The ED would make all efforts to track the money."

After chatting for some more time, they went to the kitchen to fix dinner.

* * * * *

Chapter - XV

The following morning, Neelesh left Natasha's home at 7 am, saying he needed to reach the High Court by 10 am. He told Natasha that he would first go to his house, get ready and leave for the court.

Neelesh seemed more concerned about the missing money than Natasha. After getting ready, he went to the district court instead of the High Court. It was 10 am, and the lawyers had started occupying their respective chambers. Vikram was already at work. Neelesh entered his chamber and was about to introduce himself when Vikram got up quickly and said,

"Good morning, sir. Please come in."

"Good morning, I am Neelesh."

"I know, sir. I have seen you several times in the High Court. Do you have a matter here today?"

"Yeah, a small one," Neelesh lied. He continued, "I heard one of the accused being represented by you made allegations against officers of the Enforcement Directorate."

"Oh, that. It keeps happening."

"Yes. The clients never share everything. I also saw your name in the case of Suman Foundation vs. Cherry Hills Construction."

"Yes. It was at the P & H High Court."

"I have a matter on environmental law with me. As I was searching on the internet, I came across that judgement. You had a strong case, but it went against you."

"Yes, I think the builder managed."

"But it was before a bench, which had justice Chowdhary, who had the reputation of being upright."

"Yeah, I too was hopeful, but finally, it was dismissed on frivolous grounds."

"So, the builder used the money?"

"Sir, there were rumours that an amount of Rs 28 crore exchanged hands."

Neelesh's eyes widened and he said,

"That much?"

"Sir, it is nothing for the builder. He is making six towers each, having 90 flats. The cost of one flat would be between 4-5 crores. Rs 28 crores is just 6-7 apartments. He might have paid."

"Vinod Goyal was representing him?"

"Yeah."

"You never thought of going into the Supreme Court."

"Sir, I have never appeared before the Supreme Court so far."

Neelesh laughed and said,

"You may ask the Suman Foundation representative if they are interested. I am here. Let them file an appeal. I will appear; this case is worth fighting."

"I know they would be willing."

Neelesh got up and said,

"Let me know when it has to be done. We will be in it together."

"Sure, sir."

Courts start at 10:30 am. It was time for him to leave.

*　*　*

Raghunath and Samir were sitting in Ameya's room when Rajan Mathur, the DG, entered. They all stood up. Rajan said,

"Sit down, please."

They all sat down.

"The additional secretary was very upset. Do you know, the news is out there in all the newspapers? It reflects a bad image," the DG said.

Rajan was upset but was looking calm. They all waited.

"I have been asked to issue a small press release countering that allegation. Ameya, please take care of it."

"I'll sir," Ameya replied.

"And try to track the money or at least, we must know, whether it has gone out of India through another passenger or source or if it is still in India."

Ameya said,

"Sir, if it is the other way round?"

"What do you mean?"

"Sir, what if the information was wrong and there was only ten thousand dollars? Then we might be on a wild goose chase."

There was a pause. Rajan Mathur got up and said,

"You find a way to wriggle out and remember we have to prepare an enquiry report within 15 days. The report should not look like an eye wash."

Rajan Mathur went out. Ameya said to Raghunath and Samir,

"Use your sources to find out whether Nihal is telling the truth. Find proof to back our theory. If the money has been offshored, gather the evidence and have a plan for recovery, if it is still in India."

Raghunath said,

"But madam, if the money has been smuggled out of India and we knew about it that too goes to our discredit."

"Definitely. At least it would prove that Nihal is lying. I want all this information within a week. I want to incorporate all the efforts and the results in our enquiry report."

* * *

Both Raghunath and Samir nodded and went out.

Raghunath said,

"I'll have to talk to my informer again."

Samir was silent. Raghunath asked him,

"What are you thinking?

Samir said, "I am thinking, if there is a way Mulliani will confide in us. He has lost the money. He would also be trying to find out."

"I doubt Mulliani would help. He will not gain anything because if we somehow get the money, it will be confiscated. If he wants to have it, he will have to try and beat us," Raghunath opined.

"I was wondering what will happen to Nihal. Will Mulliani get him killed? These are dangerous people."

"I am sure he must be keeping a watch at Nihal's house."

"Why can't we start from there? We may get some lead."

"Depute two IOs to see if there is any movement."

They went to their respective seats.

After about half an hour, Samir got a call from Vidhi,

"Hey, what's on?"

"Doing some work."

"Can we go shopping in the evening today, or are you too busy?"

"I'll call you around 5 pm and let you know. What do you want to purchase?"

Vidhi laughed,

"There are several requirements a lady has, but nothing to worry about. I am not a high-maintenance wife."

"Ok, what happened to the job you were looking for. Any response?"

"I got the interview call. It's scheduled for next Wednesday."

"That's good."

"Ok, I'll be waiting for your call."

"Right then."

Samir hung up.

* * *

At least one person was sure that Nihal had played the mischief. He was, however, wondering how he could do it. He was sitting in his office. He called Prince.

"Nihal didn't show up?"

"No, sir."

"What sort of lock is there on the door?"

"There is a latch and a medium size brass lock over it."

"We cannot open it."

"We need to have the keys, and if you allow, I can get someone to make a duplicate key."

Mulliani thought over it and said,

"Let us wait. The ED people might be roaming around. You keep a watch from a distance."

"Right, sir."

As Prince was about to go out, Mulliani called,

"Prince."

"Yes, sir."

"On that night, when Nihal went in with the trolley, you were there?"

"Yes, sir."

"And you saw him going in?"

"Yes, sir, I even have taken the picture when he showed his documents to the security personnel at the gate."

"Show me."

Prince looked at his phone, scanned it for a few seconds and showed him the picture. Nihal was there with both suitcases, showing his passport to security at the gate. Mulliani zoomed in and looked at Nihal's face. It was a natural photograph. Mulliani asked Prince to forward the same to him.

* * *

When Natasha reached the office, Sukhdev was already sitting in her cabin. She placed her purse on the side cabinet and sat down.

"Good morning, madam. It was in the news today."

"What was in the news?"

"Officers of the ED arrested a man named Nihal Singh on Monday night for carrying ten thousand US dollars, but he stated in the court the money in the suitcases was three million US dollars." "I know that."

"What?"

"Yes, Neelesh was in the court during the proceedings, and he told me what happened."

Sukhdev smiled and said,

"The Magistrate gave bail to Nihal. That dilutes…."

Before he could complete it, Natasha said,

"Neelesh didn't tell me that Nihal was granted bail!"

"Yes."

"But Neelesh told me the Magistrate ordered a further enquiry to enlarge the area of investigation."

Sukhdev placed the newspaper in front of Natasha and said,

"Please read this."

Natasha started reading the article. It was running into three columns. It took her ten minutes to finish reading. The issue was clear. Nihal secured bail and the Magistrate ordered a thorough investigation to the ED. It appeared more on the lines of a departmental enquiry. The case was diluted. Granting unconditional bail to Nihal meant he was scoot-free. But she wondered why Neelesh didn't tell her in exact terms, particularly about Nihal's bail. She said,

"Sukhdev, the suitcases contain three million dollars. I know that. You know that. Mulliani knows that…."

"Madam, we can't be sure that Mulliani knows that…"

"But you only told me that people in this trade are true to their word."

"But why would Nihal say that it contained three million dollars if he had not seen it or he had not been told so?"

"I think Mulliani must have told him. He took advantage of that information in the court and put the ED on the defensive."

"Look, the ED means the government. As accused's statement, whether right or wrong, one cannot corner the government."

"That's right madam. What would you tell Archit sir?"

Natasha had almost forgotten that she told Sukhdev it was company money. She said,

"I have already briefed him. The concern is to not be on the EDs radar. With Nihal getting the bail, I think the direction of the investigation will change. I will apprise him." She stopped for a while and said,

"Have you met Mulliani again? He is perhaps the only person who knows the truth."

"Yes, but I am avoiding meeting him until the situation cools down."

She nodded. Sukhdev got up and went out. Natasha felt something was amiss in how Neelesh behaved the previous night. She called to check on him.

"Hello," said Natasha.

"Yes, Natasha," Neelesh said.

"Are you busy? Can we talk?" Natasha asked.

"Yes, yes."

"Why didn't you tell me yesterday that he got bail?"

Neelesh didn't hesitate and then said,

"It's better to not talk about this on the phone."

Natasha realized the mistake and said, "Please come. We have to talk."

"Sure," Neelesh responded.

* * * * *

Chapter - XVI

Nihal was staying with Pratap. He had asked Pratap to arrange a new phone and a sim card. Pratap showed up at his workplace as usual to avoid any suspicion. Nihal resisted the urge to go to his own house, but he was apprehensive that Mulliani's men or the ED officers would be around there. So, he decided to stay away.

* * *

Raghunath met Topaz, his informer, again at the parking of Appollo Hospital. As Topaz sat in the car beside Raghunath, Raghunath said,

"You must have heard the story. I mean all that happened in the court?"

"Yes, sir. From the beginning, I told you the suitcases had three million dollars."

"Ok. I've heard that many times, and I trust you. Just tell me, where has the money vanished?"

"Only Nihal can tell you that. He seems to be the one who turned things around. He narrated the story in court to make his stand clear that Mulliani handed him three million dollars. The amount was there before the ED officers, and what happened after that was not in his knowledge."

"Topaz, I was there at the spot. The two suitcases were opened in front of me and other officers. It had only ten thousand dollars."

Topaz kept quiet and said,

"That is baffling. Can you talk to Mulliani?"

"Yes, I can, but what'll be the benefit?" Raghunath asked.

"There might be some missing link."

"Is it possible that money might have gone out through some other source?"

"No, Mulliani is annoyed. Everything should have been calm if the transfer had taken place through some other channel. But it is not."

"In other words, the money is still in India."

"Definitely."

Raghunath couldn't extract anything worthwhile. Topaz opened the door and said,

"I must not be seen with you. I am going."

He quickly walked away.

* * *

Neelesh called Vinod Goyal at Chandigarh.

"Hello,"

"Yes, sir, how are you?" Vinod asked,

"I am fine. What is happening in that case?"

"Which one?"

"That ALTARA brand, I was representing Kenmore Pvt. Ltd."

"Oh yes, I remember, sir. So, what have you decided?"

"Ask your client to withdraw the application from Trade Mark Authority."

"So, you agreeing to compromise?"

"No."

Vinod needed clarification, so he said,

"What do you mean?"

"Look, do you remember that case of Suman Foundation vs Cherry Hills Construction, which you got in favour of the builder? Can you recollect?"

"Yes, what has that got to do?"

"Suman Foundation has agreed to go to the Supreme Court. I'll be representing them. You were able to manage that at the High Court. Let me see how you'll manage it at the Supreme Court."

Vinod got silent, Neelesh continued,

"See, I have also learnt the amount of money that exchanged hands. Do you want to hear?"

"What do you want?"

"You withdraw the registration application of ALTARA brand, and I'll not file an appeal in the Supreme Court. That is how we can arrive at a compromise."

Vinod thought for a moment and said,

"What are we going to gain by this settlement?"

Neelesh laughed loudly and said,

"Easy, you tell your client at Cherry Hill that Suman Foundation is going into appeal before the Supreme Court and that you can stop that, which will cost them. I tell my client Kenmore Pvt. Ltd. that your client is ready for settlement, but that will cost them. You take your money, and I take mine."

"Smart," said Vinod Goyal and continued.

"Let me think."

"Sure, take your time. You convince Cherry Hills Constructions, and I convince Kenmore Pvt. Ltd. It is not only in our interest but also in their interest." "Give me a day," said Vinod, and they hung up.

* * *

Raghunath couldn't resist the temptation of meeting Mulliani. He had a feeling that Mulliani was responsible for all these problems. He initiated it by acting on the information. Though, as an Assistant Director of the ED, it was not prudent on his part to visit a Hawala operator, he decided to visit Mulliani nonetheless.

It took Raghunath over an hour to reach Mulliani's shop in Kirti Nagar. Finally, he located it.

Ravi Chohan saw him entering. He could judge by his experience the visitor was some government official. He stood up.

"Yes, sir, how can I help you?"

"Is Mr Mulliani there?"

"I'll check, sir. Please be seated."

"It's alright."

Ravi went down, and when he came up, Mulliani was with him. On seeing Raghunath, Mulliani said,

"I am Mulliani."

"Raghunath from …"

"Oh, sir, I know. Please come. Are you here to buy something?"

Raghunath smiled and said,

"No, you know why I am here?"

"Sir, let's sit in my office." Then he looked at Ravi and said, "Please send tea in my room."

It was a small cabin in the basement, a par for the course for any shopkeeper. Once tea was served, Mulliani said,

"Sir, I have seen you in the ED office."

"Mulliani, I am not here in any official capacity. I have come to have an informal chat." Raghunath looked around, Mulliani said,

"Sir, don't worry. There is no camera here. No listening device. Nothing of that sort. We can talk."

"Yes, sure?"

"Yes, sir."

"You may be wondering why I am here."

Mulliani smiled and said, "Sir, perhaps it is related to Nihal's case. I have learnt the court has ordered an investigation regarding Nihal's confession in the court."

"Three million US dollars?"

Mulliani smiled and kept quiet. Raghunath said,

"How much cash was there in those two suitcases?"

"Sir, your officers had recorded my statement the other day. At the end of the statement, it was written that it was voluntary without any threat or coercion."

"And you had stated ten thousand US dollars simply to corroborate what was recovered and what Nihal had initially admitted."

"That was my voluntary statement."

"Mulliani, I assure you there is nothing official about my visit here today. Nothing you share will be on record. I know you handed him over three million dollars. That amount was being transferred to your counterpart in Dubai, but your man, Nihal, duped you. Look, we are mature people. Let us help each other."

Mulliani got serious, but he was still suspicious. He said,

"What sort of help?" He continued, "Sir, doesn't it look strange that an Assistant Director from the ED is seeking help from me? You suspect me of sending the three million dollars?"

"We don't suspect that. We know that your admission in this casual one-on-one chat will not go against you in any manner. We will behave in future as if we had not met today," Raghunath said reassuringly.

"Sir, you are a senior government employee. You have to enforce rules and regulations and catch the offender. I belong to a different world. There is no agreement, no contract, no voucher or no receipts. We honour the spoken word. You don't," Mulliani said defensively.

Raghunath listened to him. Mulliani was right. Raghunath knew that on the other side of the law, the unwritten rule is the word of mouth. He said,

"But today, I give you my word. Nothing will happen to you, particularly in Nihal's case."

"Where is Nihal?"

"What sort of question is this? He is out on bail."

"After bail, he has not been seen. Can you tell me where he might be hiding?"

Raghunath was surprised. He said,

"Hadn't he met you?"

"He wouldn't come near me if he cared for his life."

Mulliani's last words were sufficient to suggest that Nihal had certainly duped him. As he expected, the money changing hands was three million dollars.

Raghunath smiled and said,

"Thank you, Mulliani. You conveyed what …"

"Where is he?" Mulliani asked.

"I don't know. Nihal's lawyer had come to the ED office to take away his passport."

Now, it was Mulliani's turn to get shocked,

"Did Vikram come to get his passport released? When?"

"Yes, on the same day when he was granted bail." Raghunath paused for a moment and said,

"I am not sure what was the name of the lawyer. My junior came and said that Nihal's lawyer had come to get his passport released."

Mulliani picked up his phone, scanned it and showed Ragunath a picture of a man.,

"This is his lawyer, Vikram. Did he come to the ED office?"

"I told you I didn't see the person."

"Can you get it confirmed?"

Raghunath smiled and said,

"Yes, I can. I'll have to make a call, but you have to promise that you'll help me."

"If it was Vikram. I am with you. Unofficially."

"Yes, of course."

"No one else will ever know about this meeting."

Raghunath finally said, "Oh, come on, the knowledge of this meeting would reflect adversely on me. Not on you." He took out his phone and called Dinesh, the IO, talked for a minute and disconnected the call. Then he looked at Mulliani and said,

"Yes, it was Vikram."

Mulliani got lost in his thoughts. Raghunath, too preferred, to remain quiet. He kept looking at Mulliani. Finally, Mulliani took a deep breath and said,

"Yes, it was three million dollars. But as I said, our job is based on word of mouth. If I promised a client he would get delivery in Dubai, they will. It'll be me who is going to bear the loss."

"That much loss?"

"It is a business. When there is gain, there is loss, too."

"Mulliani, if our department can track and recover the money, it will become government property. I cannot help you in getting the money back. I am sure you are quite aware of that."

"Yes."

"You are correct that there is no reason for you to help us recover the money."

"There is a reason."

"What?"

"I don't want that money to go to Nihal. I would prefer it goes to the government instead. I am sure he has the money because he bought my lawyer. I cannot find the answer to 'how?' You ensure you'll track the money and leave the punishment to me. I know how to punish such people."

"I will do my best."

"Nihal had not come to his house."

"He might have left the country."

"He may leave in the next few days if he hid the money somewhere. Have you been to his house?"

"No." Raghunath was surprised. They should have done it by now.

"His house is locked. I've been told that your officers might be watching his house. I can get the lock open."

"Wait. I'll get it opened officially in the presence of witnesses. Do you suspect that money would be in his house?"

"No. That is not possible. Since Nihal had the two suitcases, he had not entered the flat. But a clue or a lead may be there."

Raghunath got up. He shook hands with Mulliani and said,

"Why don't you leave this job of money transfer? You have such a good shop at such a good market."

Mulliani laughed and said, "Sir, you are there because we are here." They came upstairs. Raghunath glanced at a few pieces of furniture and came out.

157

* * * * *

Chapter - XVII

When Vikram received the call, Neelesh was sitting with Vikram to discuss the matter of the Suman Foundation. It was Nihal. Though Neelesh couldn't hear what exactly Nihal was saying, he could make out that Nihal was seeking two more days to pay his fees. Once Vikram hung up on him, Neelesh could get it that Vikram helped Nihal get his passport. This indicated that Nihal must be paying more than Mulliani to Vikram. Neelesh told Vikram to prepare the appeal on specific grounds countering the points raised in the High Court for discussing the PIL. He spent another 15 minutes with Vikram and came out. He instructed Kishan,

"Let us go to the High Court."

"Ok, sir."

Kishan moved the vehicle. Neelesh was sure that all the money was with Nihal and that he was looking for an opportunity to leave the country. But the question that remained unanswered was how did Nihal get the money. He kept thinking. Neelesh, at the moment, had no interest in meeting Natasha, but he had promised her. He looked at the watch. It was 4 pm. He thought he would decide later about that. Neelesh had a friend who was the station manager of Air India. His name was Prashant. Neelesh had once obliged Prashant in a property matter. He called Prashant.

"Hello,"

"Yes," Prashant was on the other side.

"Prashant, I am…"

"Oh, hello, Neelesh; how come you called today? How is everything?"

"I am fine. How are things at your end?"

"All good."

"Are you still an Air India?"

"Yeah. No other airline will give me a job."

"Don't say that. I need to know something about a case I am handling."

"I'll be happy if I am of any help."

Neelesh asked him about Monday night's flight of Air India Express scheduled at 11.20 pm from New Delhi to Dubai and asked whether any passenger was offloaded. Prashant was a little curious. He asked,

"Why? What happened?"

"Nothing. I am working on a case. The person said he travelled to Dubai on that flight. I am interested in whether it is some alibi or he was in Delhi.

"What's the name of the passenger?"

"Prashant, you just find out if there was any offloading. If there was, please get the details and inform me. That much information would help me in building my case."

"I think it will not be difficult."

They disconnected. Neelesh was making a vague sequence of events. If Nihal had gone inside the departure hall with two suitcases full of three million dollars given by Natasha, did someone else come out with those suitcases? Dealing with criminals for a long time, Neelesh had to think one step ahead of them. Kishan dropped Neelesh at gate no. 3 of the High Court and drove towards parking.

* * *

Raghunath was back in his office. He discussed with Samir about meeting his informer and Mulliani. Samir was surprised,

"You went to meet Mulliani?"

"Yes,"

"Sir, are you taking it personally?"

Raghunath ignored his remark and said,

"He confessed having sent three million dollars."

"Really?"

"Yes. Now it is from the horse's mouth."

"That means Nihal…."

"Yes, and Nihal has disappeared after bail, and he also has his passport with him."

"He must have left the country?"

"As per Mulliani, Nihal is in India and money is somewhere here. The question that bothers him is how Nihal pulled this stunt."

"Mulliani must be very angry with Nihal?"

"Angry? He is ready to kill him. He is keeping a watch at Nihal's residence."

"Shall we tell Ameya madam?"

"She is already annoyed. She won't believe me. What is needed is to recover the money. Anything less than that would not satisfy her."

"So, we have to find out the answer to Mulliani's big question 'How'?"

"Yes, Samir, we have not visited Nihal's house yet. Don't you think we should have done that as a standard practice?"

"Sir, we normally do that. But in this case, the recovery was less, and the person concerned was in our custody since interception."

"Do it now?"

"But will there be anybody in the house?"

"It is locked. Take two witnesses, break the lock and search the premises. There could be a possibility of some clues."

"When?"

"Do it today."

Samir looked at the watch. It was 5 pm. He recollected Vidhi's call, but he didn't want to offend. Moreover, the whole exercise would not take more than one hour. He was not expecting anything during the search.

* * *

Mulliani was annoyed at Vikram. Vikram never told him that Nihal's passport was released, particularly when he instructed Vikram to keep Nihal's release in abeyance till he reached the court. That meant Vikram kept lying to Mulliani that Nihal was already released from the prisoner's lock up at the court. In contrast, Nihal was always with Vikram and Vikram went to the ED office, got Nihal's passport released and handed it over to Nihal. Nihal definitely must have made Vikram a handsome offer. Mulliani's primary focus was Nihal. He knew he would handle Vikram later on. But Mulliani was so frustrated at the thought of two of his trustworthy persons deceiving him.

* * *

The ED officers broke the door of Nihal's flat to search the premises. Samir and three IOs were present with a search warrant duly signed by Raghunath. This time Samir, was cautious to bring with them two witnesses to avoid any embarrassment.

It was a one-room apartment. There was a bed in one corner of the room. Four chairs and a central table at another corner, a wooden almirah built on one of the walls was not locked. It had a few of Nihal's clothes. The bed had no box. The IOs looked under the bed. It was empty.

Samir entered the kitchen. The tiny place had some unused utensils lying in haphazardly on the shelf. There was no almirah or cupboard in the kitchen.

That was all. Samir called Raghunath and said,

"Sir, there is nothing."

"It was expected. The money was not there. Are there any documents?"

"Documents?" Samir laughed.

"Anything that could connect with his travelling. Anything like tickets, some currency purchase receipts or bank documents."

"No, sir. We have seen. There is nothing."

"Ok. Prepare a *panchnama* and come back," Raghunath said.

An IO started preparing the document. Samir kept roaming in the room casually. Suddenly, he saw a plastic waste basket. There were some torn papers. He poured all the contents on the floor. There were two tags of Desley brand suitcases. He picked those. These appeared to have been cut from the suitcases. He looked through the papers. It was the purchase receipt of two Desley suitcases. from the day when Nihal was intercepted. Samir handed over the torn receipts and the tags to the IO, who was preparing the *panchnama* and asked him to incorporate the recovery of those.

The proceedings concluded at about 6:30 pm. Samir called Vidhi and told her that he could be back home by 7 pm and that they could go shopping if the shops were still open.

* * *

Neelesh reached Natasha's house in Gurugram at 8:30 pm and asked Kishan to go home. Natasha had already been at her home.

She opened the door with a smile on her face and hugged him. Neelesh said,

"Happy to see you smiling. Keep smiling."

"After talking with Sukhdev and reading the news about the court proceeding, I feel relaxed."

Neelesh thought he had to be cautious in whatever he was to talk.

"That is good. It gives me pleasure when I see you in a relaxed mood. How was your day?"

"Great. After many days, I was in my usual form. What will you have?" Natasha said, pointing towards a mini bar at the side corner.

"Anything of your choice."

They both started drinking. Natasha ordered some food online. She asked,

"Mulliani must have been very angry with Nihal."

"Who is Mulliani?" Neelesh said.

"I told you the whole story the other day. I told you that Sukhdev had met him and handed over the money to him. You are forgetting the things."

"Oh, I did forget. There are so many other things occupying the mind. Yeah, Mulliani may be annoyed."

"Will he be harmed?"

"Who?"

"Nihal. I have heard these people are dangerous."

"Oh dear, why are you worried? These things keep happening. We lawyers get cases because criminals are there."

"But that was my money."

Neelesh thought over the statement made by Natasha. He slowly said,

"You said that you were not concerned with the money. Your fear was more about the ED approaching you."

"Yes, I am not concerned about money anymore. But still, once in a while, it keeps coming at the back of the mind. It was a huge amount of money."

Neelesh took a sip and said,

"The best for you is to forget the money. As if nothing of this sort ever occurred in your life."

"You are right." She said and cuddled into Neelesh's arms, but she felt no warmth, she felt no excitement. She didn't know the reason.

* * *

Prince and Jaydev saw the enforcement officers leaving Nihal's flat. There was nothing in their hand except one file. After the officers went away, both Prince and Jaydev climbed the stairs. The door of Nihal's house was locked and sealed with a government seal. Prince called Mulliani,

"Sir, the officers from the ED were here at Nihal's house. They remained here for about an hour, but left without any recovery."

"Ok," Mulliani said thoughtfully.

"They have sealed the door when they left," Prince said.

"It's all right. That must be their standard drive. There is no sign of Nihal?"

"No, sir."

"Both of you can keep visiting the place for a few more days."

"Right, sir."

They disconnected. It was as expected. The money would have never made it to Nihal's home. Mulliani was annoyed with Vikram. He had trusted Vikram to handle the cases about money transfers. Two small matters were handed over to him, which Vikram had completed. There was no reason for Vikram to betray him. But this time, Vikram had lied to him that Nihal was released and left the court, whereas the fact was that Nihal was with Vikram throughout that day. Mulliani had underestimated Nihal. Nihal had overpowered Vikram and the only possibility could be the promise of money. "Promise" because Nihal was just released that day. He had no money to pay Vikram yet. As far as Vikram was concerned, there must have been a strong and reliable reason to trust a man like Nihal.

He thought Vikram needed to be taught a lesson for this betrayal, but that could wait.

*　*　*　*　*

Chapter - XVIII

A core group meeting was going on in Archit's room. Mukul Sharma, an independent director in the company, was in attendance. The plant head was there, along with two VPs. Natasha was present. Archit started the meeting by addressing everyone present.

He said, "Olympic Paints (India) Pvt. Ltd. is a big name in Paints Industries. I was looking at last quarter's turnover. It has gone down. Have any of you noticed?"

"Yes, sir. It has drastically come down." Natasha said she was the one to keep track of the sales. All figures came to her and she consolidated them and forwarded them to the MD in her report. The drop in the revenue was a matter of concern, but knowing the reasons behind it was not part of her role. Archit looked at the VP (marketing) and said,

"Our sales have dipped. What can be the reasons behind this?"

The VP (Marketing), Vishnu Mohanti, was on the verge of retirement. Mohanti said,

"Sir, many new companies have flooded the markets, selling paint at cheaper rates. We are competing with those."

"Look, their customers must be interested in buying cheaper products but we target high-end customers. We are not competing with them," Archit said.

"We are, sir. Their quality may not be as good. I can't comment on that. But we are importing major raw materials from abroad. The rupee keeps taking a dip against the dollar, and we keep paying more for the procurement of materials. Moreover, these small companies do not pay taxes. Tax rate is 18 percent. Adding this with an increase in the exchange rate, makes our product 25 percent dearer compared to theirs. Our infrastructure cost and overheads are more. The cumulative effect increases our cost by more than 30 and that is a big amount," Mohanti replied.

"How was it then that we were performing well in the last quarters?" Archit asked.

"We were somehow managing?" Mohanti responded.

"We cannot afford to lower the quality of our products. Nor can we sell the goods without paying taxes. What is the alternative?" Archit enquired. Vishnu said, "We need to explore more and more export markets. We don't have to pay taxes on exports. The foreign buyers want good quality products. Our quality matches international standards."

The discussion went on. More and more suggestions poured in. Archit's main thrust was to increase sales without compromising quality. The meeting wrapped up an hour later. When everybody was leaving, Archit signaled to Natasha to stay back. Once they were alone, Archit asked,

"Have you checked the figures properly? I don't remember losing any major clients. Orders are also coming regularly."

"I'll check and recheck," Natasha said.

"Yeah, is it a sales dip or a profit dip? You know I want to be doubly sure before sharing this data with the foreign directors," Archit said.

"Sure, sir," Natasha said.

Archit opened the drawer and took out an envelope. It looked like an invitation card. He gave it to Natasha and said,

"Natasha, the Haryana Chamber of Commerce and FICCI are organizing a seminar at the FICCI auditorium on Saturday. Look at this."

Natasha opened the envelope. It was a day-long program. The subject was related to practical difficulties being faced by importers and exporters. The various relaxations given by RBI and FEMA will be highlighted. Many eminent speakers were invited to speak. Archit said,

"I am nominating you as a delegate. The aim is to interact with CFOs of other companies. Meet them, as such networking sometimes helps enlarge the business prospect."

"Sure, sir, I will attend."

"How are you otherwise?"

"I've moved on a bit."

"That's good."

Natasha got up and went out.

* * *

Neelesh was on his way to the court when his phone rang. It was Prashant.

"Good morning," Prashant said.

"Good morning. How are you?" Neelesh asked.

"I am fine. Sir, I checked the Air India Express's manifest for the flight you had asked me."

"Yes," Neelesh seemed interested.

"A passenger named Pratap Singh was offloaded. His name was later on deleted from the passenger's list."

"Any reason for offloading?"

"No remarks are given."

"Was he carrying any baggage?"

"Yes, he was carrying two suitcases. To mention the number of baggages has been made mandatory, even for passengers who do not travel, for security reasons. The security personnel at the gate should record the number of baggages."

"Can I get Pratap's address?"

Prashant was getting curious,

"You are to verify his alibi, you told me. You must have his address."

"No, he is a witness from the opposite side. I have to demolish this witness. It is important. Is he from Delhi or outside Delhi?"

"Sir, to be exact, I have not checked the address."

"Prashant, please do that also. It will be a big help."

"I'll have to see; passport details are not always mentioned. First, I need to check whether this man booked the ticket directly from Air India or was it done through some travel agent."

"So, will you be able to find out?"

"Ok. Give me some time."

They disconnected.

Neelesh's doubt seemed to be correct. Pratap Singh was also carrying two suitcases and he did not travel. He came out. Yes, this would be the man.

* * *

Raghunath was looking at the tags of the suitcases and the torn purchase voucher, which were recovered from Nihal's house. He said to Samir,

"The suitcases which were detained from Nihal were of which brand?"

"They are from the same brand, Desley."

"That means he purchased these suitcases, filled them with old clothes and gave them to Mulliani, who must have hidden the currency under these clothes."

"Yes sir, it so appears."

"The date of purchase is also the same as the day of the travel."

Samir shrugged. Raghunath didn't find anything worth which could be shared with Mulliani. It had become a puzzle. As if at the same time, there was a ring on Samir's phone. It was Vidhi. He excused himself and came out, he said,

"Yes, Vidhi.

"We brought the bedsheet yesterday. I opened the packet and found that it is not the one we had chosen at the time of purchase."

"How come this happens?"

"I think there was another customer. As the packing and carrying bags are similar, it looks as if the two packets got mixed up."

"Mixed up."

"I mean exchanged," Vidhi said,

Samir put his hand on his forehead and said,

"We have to go again to that shop."

"You need not go. I'll go myself. I have the purchase receipt and bring the right bed sheet."

"Ok."

They disconnected. Samir was walking briskly towards Raghunath's room when it suddenly occurred to him, "EXCHANGED". He stopped outside Raghunath's room and started thinking. Was it possible that Nihal had exchanged the suitcases with some co-passenger? Yes, it could be possible. He immediately went to meet Raghunath in his cabin, visibly excited. He said,

"Sir, there is a possibility and perhaps the only possibility to solve the puzzle."

"Which puzzle, Samir?"

"Where the suitcases having three million dollars have disappeared."

"Yes, what is it?" Raghunath said.

"Sir, Nihal had definitely exchanged the suitcases with some other passenger."

"But we were there, keeping a surveillance."

"Sir, we didn't have an identity on Nihal. It was when he reached the check-in counter we were able to identify him. We do not know what he did between the time he entered and he reported at the counter. It could be easy. Simply pick up another baggage trolley and stand in the queue. The trolley with suitcases having money could have been taken over by someone else."

Raghunath, who was listening carefully, said,

"It didn't occur to us earlier. Yes, it could be possible. And someone else boarded the flight with money."

"Maybe 'Yes' or maybe 'No'.

"You mean, he could have come out of departure and had not flown?"

"That is a possibility because it is unlikely that Nihal can pull strings for such a huge sum getting deposited in Dubai."

"Remember, he was to fly. He was not aware that he would be unable to board the flight," Raghunath said.

"Sir, that is another reason why the money is still in the country. He would have planned it that way."

"As per Mulliani, the money is hidden in India. Samir, can we confirm it? Find out if some passenger was offloaded. The staff of Air India would tell us. Check the CCTV footage of movement outside the departure gates. All passengers go in. No one comes out."

"Yes. Normally, no one comes out of the departure gates."

"So, if anyone is seen coming out and that too with two suitcases, he is the person we are looking for."

"I'll do it, sir. I can officially go and talk to Air India staff."

"You may take Dinesh with you."

"Sure, sir."

Samir briskly walked out. Raghunath was smiling. He had one more thing on his mind. If the suitcases that were intercepted were purchased by Nihal, then these suitcases are not the ones handed over to him by Mulliani. There could be the possibility the brands may not be same. He thought of verifying this with Mulliani. He took out his mobile phone but then preferred using his official landline. He called Mulliani three times but no one picked up. Finally, he considered revisiting Mulliani's shop, while returning home from the office.

At 6 pm before leaving the office, he once again tried to call Mulliani from the landline number. Finally, Mulliani received the call.

"Yes."

"Mulliani, I am…"

"Good evening, sir. I've recognized your voice."

"Our staff had searched Nihal's residence and a torn purchase receipt of two suitcases and two tags of 'Desley' were found."

Mulliani was listening. He strictly remembered the suitcases given to him were light blue and of VIP.

Raghunath continued,

"Do you remember the brand or the colour of the suitcases handed over to Nihal?"

"No sir," said Mulliani, slowly and continued,

"Sir, I am trying to recollect."

"You must have remembered the colour?"

"No sir. There are limited colours available. If I recollect, I will get back to you."

They disconnected. Mulliani now had an idea that the suitcases seized by officers of ED would be of 'Desley'. Raghunath was only trying to find out that if the brand or colour of suitcases given by Mulliani were different, then these were swapped. He called his source at the ED,

"Shiv,"

"Yes, sir,"

"Can you find out the colour of the suitcases which were seized from my man, Nihal?"

"No need to find out. Everyone here knows that those were of dark brown."

"Thank you."

Mulliani immediately disconnected. He scanned his phone. There was a picture of Nihal carrying the trolley while going in the departure hall. He kept looking at the picture. The suitcases were light blue. This meant Nihal had exchanged the suitcases with someone else in the departure hall. And by his experience in the trade of money transfer, Mulliani could infer the other person would not have travelled. It is not easy to handle that much cash in another country without resources. He could also make out that Nihal would have planned all this in one day. Mulliani categorically remembered that Nihal was told about the quantum of the cash he was carrying on Sunday evening. Nihal was also told the flight was scheduled to depart at 11.20 pm from Delhi on Monday. So, Nihal had one full day to plan.

Mulliani was now mobilizing his resources to find out who could be the other person responsible for hiding the money.

* * * * *

Chapter - XIX

The time was 7 pm. Samir and Dinesh reached the Air India office, located near gate no. 8 of the departure hall at terminal 3 of IGI Airport, New Delhi. Only two officials were present. The office hours were over, and the majority of the staff from the day shift had left. Both the officers opened the door and went inside. Samir introduced himself.

"Hello, I am Samir, SIO from the Enforcement Directorate and he is my colleague, Dinesh."

The person sitting at the desk gave them an enquiring look and disinterestedly asked,

"Yes. What can I do for you?"

"We are here for some information."

"Sir, please come tomorrow during the office hours. We are here to supervise the flights that are scheduled now."

"Sure. I can understand, but it is urgent," Samir said politely.

"I understand sir, but I am not authorized to share any information."

Samir looked at the name tag the person had on him. His name was Dushyant. Samir said,

"Mr Dushyant, we know you are busy and supervising flights is your priority. We don't want anything in writing. The information we require must be available on your system." Samir looked at the desktop before Dushyant.

"Sir…" Dushyant said.

"We need information on a person who was offloaded from a New Delhi to Dubai flight."

The landline on Dushyant's desk was ringing continuously. He couldn't attend the calls. Finally, he said,

"Ok. Please give me the date and time of the flight."

Samir gave him the details. Dushyant started clicking the keyboard and took about 10 minutes to pull the details on his screen. Dushyant said,

"Here it is, sir. One passenger."

Samir bent a little forward and looked at the screen. He asked Dinesh to note down the details. After noting it down, Dinesh asked,

"Do you have the address of this passenger?"

"No, sir."

"What about his ticket details?" You have the PNR number. We can get the details from there."

Dushyant scanned a little bit and asked Dinesh to note down the number. Both thanked Dushyant and came out. They smiled at each other. Samir looked at the details. He said,

"So, Pratap Singh, we have a name but not the address."

"I doubt the PNR number will give us further information, Dinesh said."

"Let us go to the security people."

"They won't be that co-operative."

"Yes. Wait. I'll talk to Raghunath, sir. He can get this done."

Samir called Raghunath and spoke for a few minutes before disconnecting. Raghunath told Samir that he would get back. Meanwhile, Dinesh opened the Air India website on his phone and inserted the PNR number, but the details of the earlier flight were unavailable.

In the next five minutes, both were sitting before the officer in-charge of security on duty. Samir briefed him about the details which were required. A sub-inspector escorted them to a room where the CCTV footage was recorded. The sub-inspector talked to the officer sitting in that room. Samir had asked for the pictures captured outside the departure gates from the date of the arrest to be pulled out. It took about one hour for the officer to find the pictures.

Both Samir and Dinesh kept looking. Passengers holding the trollies were going in. It took them another hour to scrutinize the pictures and video. After about one hour, they could see a person coming out of the departure hall holding a trolley carrying two suitcases. Since the pictures were black and white, they could not ascertain the colour of the suitcases but could make out the two suitcases were not the same in size. After a few minutes, an Uber approached the passenger and they loaded the suitcases in the boot and drove away.

Samir looked at Dinesh. Both took a deep breath and came out. Before coming out, Dinesh had copied the relevant pictures and videos. Samir said,

"So, the things are getting clearer. Raghunath sir's informer was right. Nihal is the real culprit."

"Yes, sir," Dinesh said.

"So, what next?"

"To find the cab who took our man, Pratap."

Both looked at each other and smiled.

*　*　*

Mulliani often indulged people who he thought would be helpful in the future. About a month back, a couple had come to see furniture at his store. Ravi was the person taking care of them. The couple wanted a dining table with eight chairs. The one they liked was way above their budget. The wife was insisting they buy it. Mulliani was coming up from his office in the basement when he noticed them. The man's face looked familiar. Mulliani went near them and asked Ravi,

"Any issues?"

"No, sir. Nothing. They are choosing the dining table and I am showing them the various options."

Mulliani smiled and placed his hand on the dining table. He said to the lady,

"You liked this one?"

"Yes, but it is expensive."

Mulliani looked at the gentlemen and said,

"Sir. Your face looks familiar. Have we met earlier?"

"No, we have not."

"Maybe it just occurred to me."

"I worked at airport authority. You might have seen me there."

"Oh, yes. I can recollect. Once my luggage got mishandled and I think you were the person who helped me a lot that day."

"So, have you got your luggage?"

"Yes, sir. I am thankful to you."

Mulliani made the couple sit and offered them tea. Finally, Mulliani sold the dining table to them at a discounted price and the couple went happily. At the time of going, the man gave Mulliani his business card.

Mulliani searched for the card. It was there in the drawer of his table. He looked at it. His name was Anil Mehra. Mulliani called him,

"Yes, who is it?" The voice at the other end asked.

"Good evening, sir. I am Mulliani. You and your wife had bought a dining table from my shop," Mulliani said.

"Oh yes. How are you Mr Mulliani?"

"I am fine. I needed a little help."

"Yes, please tell me."

Mulliani made up a story that someone he knew was going to Dubai, carrying two suitcases but somehow misplaced one. He requested, "I was wondering if you could help me?"

"When?" It was 5-6 days back," Mulliani continued.

"Yeah, I know, it is difficult, but if you could access the CCTV footage of that day…"

"Those are managed by security people Mr Mulliani."

"But sir, the airport authority installed the cameras inside the departure hall. It is your property. If you could please help."

"Let me see if I can do anything.

"Thank you so much, sir."

Mulliani called Prince and Jaydev next. He said,

"Do you know any of Nihal's friends?"

Both shrugged their shoulders in negative and said,

"No, sir."

"Think harder; you three were friends. Is there any other person from his neighbourhood or his hometown? There must be someone. Perhaps you must have seen him hang out with someone?"

Jaydev said, "There is a man who works at a shopping mall in Rajouri Garden from his hometown. However, I am not aware if they are close."

"What is his name?" Mulliani asked.

"Sir, I do not know. Once, I was in the shopping mall with Nihal and we happened to meet that person.

"Can you recognize him?"

"Yes, definitely, sir. You want me to go to that shopping mall? It is a chance I can take."

"If we get access to the CCTV footage, will you be able to recognize him in that?"

"Perhaps, yes."

Mulliani smiled and said,

"Let's hope we get hold of some pictures from the CCTV. If we don't get it, you may visit the shopping mall and take a chance."

"Right, sir."

Mulliani looked at both Prince and Jaydev and said,

"It is vital to find out this man. In all likelihood, he is the person who is hiding our money."

Both Jaydev and Prince nodded.

* * *

Neelesh was back at his home. He was eager to find out the address of Pratap Singh. He wanted to grab the money. It was a huge amount. Neelesh, was a good person, but he knew that as a professional, he would never to able to make that much money. Unlawfully grabbing someone's money is theft, but his greed had taken over his better judgement. He knew that everyone had greed but there was a line, and when greed crossed that line, the person became a criminal. Neelesh's greed was about to cross that line.

While he was lost, deep in his thoughts, his phone started ringing. It was Prashant. His reflexes were quick.

"Yes,"

"Sir, I have got Pratap Singh's address from the travel agent who booked his ticket."

"Oh, thank you so much."

"Sir, I am just sending it to you on WhatsApp."

"Thank you once again."

As he hung up, the message came on his WhatsApp. Neelesh looked at it. Pratap was staying at Moti Nagar. It was an area in West Delhi. He checked on Google Maps; it would take him 50 minutes to reach. He decided to visit the following morning.

* * *

Samir and Dinesh visited Uber's office in Gurugram. They were doubtful if, at that hour, anybody would be available. The office looked deserted. The guard sitting outside stopped them from entering. As Dinesh was about to argue with the guard, Samir saw a man in his early forties coming out of the office. He was wearing a card displaying Uber's logo. Samir quickly approached and introduced himself. They talked for five minutes and then the person walked away. Dinesh asked,

"What happened?"

"The office is closed. He was the last person leaving. But he has given Prateek's contact number, who is in charge."

"Let's talk to him."

"Yeah, let us go and sit in the car."

Once inside the car, Samir called Prateek.

"Hello,"

"Yes, who is it?" The voice on the other side asked.

"Mr Prateek?" Samir asked.

"That's right."

"My name is Samir. I am from the Enforcement Directorate. My colleague and I are outside your office. I am sorry to call you at this hour but there is an urgent enquiry."

Prateek's voice toned down,

"Yes, sir, what is it about?"

"Mr Prateek, it has nothing to do with you or your company. We are looking for a person who had hired a cab from your company."

"Yes, please continue. I am listening."

"Will it be possible for you to tell us about the cab driver and where the passenger was dropped? He was picked up from Terminal 3 of IGI airport on Monday."

"It is five days back?"

"Yes"

"Do you have the cab number?"

Dinesh was zooming into the picture to look for the number plate. He showed it to Samir. Samir said,

"Yes. We have a picture, but it is not very clear."

"Can you forward it to me?"

"Yeah, I am sending it."

"Sir, you will have to give me an hour or maybe a little more. Since it is five days old, it may take some time but be assured, you will get the details, as we keep data of all travel routes at least for a month. The driver's account is settled after completion of the month."

"Mr Prateek, thank you so much. Please take your own time. You have my number now with you. If you need my identification, I can forward that too."

"Yes, please, do that sir. It is the company's policy not to reveal the details, as these may go into the hands of unscrupulous persons."

"I can understand. I am sending you, and you can keep it on record and I will come and meet you one of these days."

They disconnect. Samir showed thumbs up sign to Dinesh and said,

"Let us update Raghunath sir."

* * * * *

Chapter - XX

It was Saturday morning. Since his bail, Nihal had been staying at Pratap's house. For the last two days, he wanted to look at the money in the suitcases. Moreover, Nihal needed the money to repay the loan and Vikram's fees. On Friday night, he had discussed with Pratap regarding visiting the place where the suitcases were hidden. Nihal had seen the place a couple of times when they had visited their hometown together. He had obtained the room keys from Pratap and planned a trip to Sampla.

Saturday at 9 am Nihal came out of the Pratap's house. The Uber he had booked was waiting on the left side of the road. He opened the door and sat down. The Uber driver asked for an OTP and started the ride.

Nihal was unaware that an SUV parked on the right side of the road was waiting for him. That car, too, started moving behind the Uber. The area around Moti Nagar was congested, but after about ten minutes, the car came on a highway, heading towards Rohtak.

* * * * *

PART - 3

Chapter - XXI

Saturday being the weekend, the traffic on Delhi roads was sparse. Kuku was driving the car, and Natasha sat in the back seat. They were heading to the FICCI auditorium near Mandi House.

Natasha reached her destination for the day at 10:15 am. Kuku dropped her and took the car to the parking. As Natasha entered, she saw a table where a couple of girls were sitting. They smiled at Natasha. She took out her business card. One of the girls looked at it and moved a register towards her to make an entry. It had columns like name, company, designation, email address, and mobile number. In the last column, she had to put her signatures. The girl handed Natasha a folder and delegate's card for wearing around the neck. She escorted Natasha inside the auditorium and showed the pre-allotted seat, where Natasha went and sat. Almost ninety percent of the auditorium seats were occupied. A table was arranged, on the stage where five chairs for distinguished guests were placed. None of the guests had occupied the chair yet. On the table, the name of the guests was displayed. She tried to read those. One was Mr Swaminathan, a senior advocate known to be an expert on matters of foreign exchange. Second was Ameya Mohite, Joint Director, Enforcement Directorate. The other three names were the office bearers of FICCI, who had organized the seminar.

Natasha looked around. Most of the people were sitting in formal attire. Few were chatting. She tried to look for some known face but there was no one. Meanwhile, an old lady with grey hair came, smiled at Natasha and sat on the seat next to Natasha. Natasha smiled back at her. She looked at the agenda on the back of the invitation card. There were two sessions. The first session was scheduled to start at 10:30 am and continue until 1:30 pm. There was a welcome address by the chairman of FICCI. Then a few industry experts were to speak on the subject and the difficulties being faced by the trade. Natasha counted; there were six speakers. How boring, she thought to herself. From 1:30 pm to 2:30 pm was lunch break. The second session was scheduled from 2:30 pm to 4:30 pm. It was a panel discussion and Ameya and Swaminathan were the speakers. From 4:30 pm to 5:30 pm, an hour was marked for questions and answers. From 5:30 pm to 6:30 pm was a tea break. At 6:30, there would be a vote of thanks and the seminar would be concluded.

Natasha was never interested in such seminars. It is an open secret, that the participants were only complying with the orders of their respective senior managements to attend such seminars. Lunch and tea breaks were typically meant for networking. The representatives could informally meet each other and exchange business cards. Such interaction was for the furtherance of individual interests rather than the interests of the companies being represented.

An executive from FICCI came to the stage at 10:30 am to compare. He announced the guests individually and requested them to join on the dais. Flower bouquets were offered to each one of them. After this, the chairman of FICCI got up and started his welcome address. It lasted for about ten minutes. Then the speakers started coming. Each one, no doubt was knowledgeable. Few of them were good orators. The speeches were on the Prevention of Money Laundering Act, 2002 (PMLA) and the Foreign Exchange Management Act, 1999. The first act pertains to preventing money laundering. Laundering meant washing dirty clothes. Money laundering meant the instances of converting black money into white. In other words, to clean the dirty money. The second act pertained to regulating foreign exchange. There were restrictions on the possession of foreign exchange, import and export of foreign exchange, investments outside India by Indian residents, investments in India by a foreign national and so on.

Natasha kept listening like the others. Most of the issues were known to her as she had been practically involved in such issues as CFO of a company, which was engaged in the import of raw materials and the export of manufactured goods. The last speaker of the first session finished addressing the audience at 1:20 pm. The person comparing the event announced that it was lunch break. He informed everyone that just on the right side of the auditorium was a lawn where the arrangements for lunch had been made. Soon the delegates moved towards the lawn. It was a winter afternoon. The weather was good. The delegates started meeting each other. Natasha met a couple of delegates and exchanged business cards. When the crowd started settling down with their food, Natasha, too picked up a plate and started putting some salad, yogurt, rice and a little bit of lentils. She preferred a light lunch. She saw a vacant chair and sat down. She would smile whosoever would pass by. After about ten minutes, she saw the chairman of FICCI, Swaminathan and Ameya, standing at the opposite side and chatting. She got up and went to them.

On reaching them, she smiled and bowed a little. She said,

"Natasha Chowdhary."

"Hello. I am Raman, Raman Goenka," the chairman said.

"Sir, it's nice to see you. I am from Olympic Paints." She opened the wallet, took out a card and handed it over to him. "She nodded towards Ameya, and Swaminathan. Raman was quick. He said,

"She is Ameya from the ED and he is…"

"I know, sir. Who has not heard of him? He is an institute in himself. And how nice to meet you madam." Natasha said and shook hands with both of them. She handed them her business cards. Ameya looked at the card and spoke.

"How do you feel about working in a manufacturing unit, particularly as a woman? I see very few women here."

"Oh madam, it has been now more than a decade. I joined as a chartered accountant. The management promoted me, I have been the CFO for the last four years," Natasha replied.

"That's good. I believe that more and more women should join the corporate." Ameya said.

"They are more sincere," Swaminathan said smilingly.

"Sir, is it meant as a compliment or are you making fun…" Ameya said.

"Seriously, it is a compliment."

All of them laughed. They kept chatting and in another 10 minutes, Natasha excused herself and returned to her seat in the auditorium.

The next session started at 2:30 pm. Central table was placed in the middle of the stage. Three people were sitting on the panel. Ameya, Swaminathan and Raman. They picked up the subject of regulation of foreign exchange in the country. Most of the talking was being done by Swaminathan. He shared some presentation slides when the sections of FEMA came up. Ameya made a few comments when Raman would specifically ask her. Bureaucrats are normally non-committal. Their answers can be interpreted both ways. The session and discussion continued till 4:30 pm. At the end, Raman looked towards the audience and said,

"Well, my friends from the industry, if you have any questions, you are welcome. We have with us today Mr Swaminathan and Ms Ameya. I am sure they will be happy to clarify any doubts, on today's subject."

There were a couple of sundry queries, to which Swaminathan responded and took an unnecessarily long time. Then it suddenly occurred to Natasha that she could also put up a question which was relevant to her personally. She raised her hand.

"Yes, please," Raman said.

"With due regards to the panellist, I have to say that what I have understood is the burden of proof under money laundering, that is, PMLA is on the accused and the burden of proof under Foreign Exchange regulation, that in FEMA is on the prosecution?" Natasha said.

"That's right and Ms Ameya can better tell the provisions of both the acts," Swaminathan said, looking at Ameya. Before Ameya could say anything, Natasha smiled and said,

"Sir, I am not interested in the provisions. Perhaps I'll not remember those provisions once I leave this auditorium."

There were a few laughs. Natasha continued,

"Sir, suppose I have ten thousand dollars with me, and the ED recovers this. The burden of proof will lie on whom, me or the ED?"

"If you can explain the source, it is on the ED."

"And if I cannot explain?"

"How is that possible? It is your money, it is in your possession, you cannot say that you do not know how you have acquired it," Swaminathan said.

"Agreed. But suppose I am cannot explain, or recollect, will I be penalized or prosecuted?"

Swaminathan was getting restless. He said,

"I will try to explain it with reference to Indian currency. We have the Income Tax Act. Do you file an income tax return each year?"

"Yes, sir. I do," Natasha replied.

"There are different heads to indicate the source of income. It may be salary, interest, sale of property, shares, dividends, rental, etc. You declare your income against each head, make a total and work out the tax to be paid. Am I right?"

"Right, sir."

"And if still some money is left which you have not declared or unable to declare, that becomes illegal money. I mean, any money recovered from you, the source of which cannot be explained, would be deemed to have been acquired illegally. The same applies to your ten thousand dollars. If you cannot explain its source, it is illegal. Simple."

"But, sir...."

Ameya interrupted.

"Don't worry, the ED will not prosecute you for ten thousand dollars."

Natasha hesitated for a moment, then said,

"Madam, the question may look hypothetical. Suppose it is more money, say a million dollars. The basic principle shall be the same. What is the remedy? Is there any method under FEMA where I can declare the money voluntarily without fear of any punitive action? As Swaminathan sir, pointed out in the Income Tax Act, if the source is not explainable, I can always declare it without fear. I think no parallels can be drawn. Can I do the same under FEMA?"

"I am afraid not," Ameya said thoughtfully. Raman was hearing all this. He felt the issue was getting unnecessarily stretched. He said to Ameya,

"Madam, sometimes the questions are asked to see how the authorities react. Let us see if there is any other question."

Natasha said,

"Sir, I am not trying to see how Ameya madam reacts. I am trying to gain knowledge. I have had an opportunity through this seminar to clear certain doubts. And sir, I will not take more than five minutes. Please allow me."

Raman looked at Swaminathan and Ameya both. Swaminathan said,

"Madam, I am sorry I have not understood the real issue so far…"

Natasha said,

Sir, I have a certain quantity of US dollars. I do not know the source. I cannot spend it. I cannot keep it. I cannot declare it. Spending, keeping, declaring or even sharing with someone amounts to an offence. Am I right, Ameya madam?"

Ameya kept quiet. Natasha said,

"Sir, let us say it's a windfall. I suddenly lay hands on a large quantity of foreign currency. I do not want to keep it. I do not want to spend my life in guilt or fear. I am sure there must be some law to save an innocent citizen?"

Raman laughed and said,

"What's your name, madam?"

"Natasha, Natasha Chowdhary."

"Oh yes, we met during lunch break. Let's hope everyone gets such windfall once in their lifetimes. How fortunate!"

The delegates started getting up. It was time for the tea break. Natasha said slowly,

"How unfortunate!"

No one listened to the last two words that came from Natasha's lips but Ameya did. They smiled at each other. Everyone came out for tea. A few delegates came to Natasha as if appreciating her question. Natasha was not very good in public speaking but she spoke well that day. It was impromptu.

Ameya, Swaminathan and Raman were talking over tea. Ameya was looking at Natasha through the corner of her eyes. She was skillful enough to read minds.

In another 10 minutes, Raman clapped and started his vote of thanks.

The photographer was busy taking pictures throughout the session. He clicked a few final group pictures. Ameya walked towards her car. Raman escorted her. While she was sitting in the car, she said,

"I hope you'll forward me a few pictures."

"Sure madam," Raman replied.

*　*　*　*　*

Chapter - XXII

On Saturday morning, Samir got up and checked his phone. There was no call or message from Prateek. So, he decided to call him instead.

"Hello,"

"Yes, sir. I am sorry, I couldn't find the location yesterday. I have called the driver of that cab at our office. At 10 am, he will be at the office, and then I'll be able to tell you the drop location you are looking for."

"I thought it would be available on your system."

"Yes, generally it is, sir, but somehow, I couldn't locate it. But before 11 am, you will get the details."

"Shall I come to your office?"

"Sir, if you wish to drop by, you are welcome. However, we will share the details with you as soon as we get them."

Samir looked at his watch. It was 8 am. He said,

"Ok. I will drop by. I want to talk to the driver."

"Welcome, sir."

Samir disconnected the call and called Dinesh to tell him they needed to go to the Uber office.

At 10:20 am, both were sitting before Prateek. Prateek told them that as per the GPS tracking, the passenger first went to some place in Sampla and then the cab returned to Delhi and dropped the passenger in Moti Nagar. Samir said,

"Can we have a word with the driver?"

"Yes," Prateek called the peon and told him to send Dilawer, the Uber driver, who was sitting outside his office. In another minute, Dilawer entered. Prateek said,

"Dilawer, they are government officers. They want to talk to you."

Dilawer looked at Samir and Dinesh.

"Yes, sir?"

Samir smiled and said,

"Dilawer, there is nothing to worry about. We need the name and number of the passenger whom you drove to Sampla from the airport and then back to Moti Nagar."

Dilawer took out his phone and tapped on the ride history. He showed it to Samir. Dinesh noted down the number.

"So, this passenger named Pratap asked you to go to Sampla and then back to Moti Nagar? Can you identify both the places?"

Dilawer said hesitantly.

"Sir Sampla, I may not be able to identify. I had never been to that place before. Moreover, it was dark. But I can tell you where I dropped him in Moti Nagar."

"Do you have his address?"

"No sir, the passenger told me to stop near a handloom shop. He made the payment in cash and went in the lane adjacent to that shop."

Samir looked at Prateek and said,

"We would like to take Dilawer with us to identify the location."

Prateek said,

"Sir, you have got his telephone number. You can find out the exact address of Pratap with GPS."

Samir and Dinesh looked at each other. Samir said,

"Pretty smart. It never occurred to us."

"Still, you can have Dilawer's number. If required, he will go and co-operate." Prateek said looking at Dilawer.

Dilawer said, "Yes, sir."

Both men got up, and once they came out, Dinesh called his office and passed on Pratap's number to the IO sitting in the system.

* * *

The cab crossed the Delhi-Haryana border and passed through the busy areas of Bahadurgarh. The traffic on the highway was chaotic. Buses were standing in the middle of the road. Tractors were moving. Cars were parked on both sides. People were crossing the road at their will. It took the driver about half an hour to come out of that patch of the highway. Nihal belonged to Sampla, so, he was well-versed with the area and the traffic conditions. He checked the time; it was 11:20 am. It took him more than two hours to cover the distance. At that time of the day, it was par for the course. But once they crossed that leg of the journey, it would take at the most 25 minutes to reach Sampla. Nihal directed the driver to take a left turn from the highway when they neared Sampla. Nihal showed the stone crusher from a distance and told the driver to go to that place. On reaching at the spot, Nihal told the driver they were to go back to Delhi and he would pay the waiting charges. The driver just smiled and parked the car on the side of the boundary wall where the crusher was installed.

Nihal went inside. He had the keys, opened the lock of the small room and entered. He kept the door slightly open as the room was not well lit. He looked under the cot and pulled the bedsheet. There were two suitcases. He smiled. He wanted to see the money with his own eyes. He looked around, closed the door and switched on his phone's flashlight.

Now, it was tricky. The suitcases were locked, and Nihal didn't know the code. He didn't want to break the locks, as they needed to keep the suitcases there for a few more days. He recollected Mulliani once talking on the phone to someone conveying the numerical code. Mulliani was in the habit of keeping repeated digits as the code, like 000 or likewise. Nihal decided to try. First, he set the code at 111. It couldn't open. Next, he set the code at 222, it again didn't open. As he was about to try 333, there was a knock at the door. Nihal pushed back both the suitcases under the cot and slowly opened the door. It was the driver.

"Yes?"

"Sir, do you have water here?"

The driver was holding an empty water bottle in his hand. Nihal shrugged and said,

"No, but there is a small market about half a kilometre from here. You can buy two bottles from there and keep one for me in the car. I will be done in another half an hour."

Nihal handed over the money to the driver to buy the water bottles. When Nihal heard the car going away, he pulled the suitcases out again. He tried opening at code 333. It opened. He excitedly looked under the clothes. Well, the money was there. He counted 15 bundles of 10 racks of US dollars in one suitcase and 15 in another. He kept looking at money. So, finally, he could lay hands on a big fortune. He looked around. The door was slightly opened. He came out. No one was there. He came out of the main gate. The cab was also not there. He was alone. He immediately went in. He opened one bundle of ten racks and pulled out two racks, which meant 20,000 US dollars. He put those in the pocket of his jacket. He placed the money and clothes back as these were. He closed the suitcases at the same numerical code, 333, and moved the number randomly. He covered the suitcases with the bedsheet. Nihal came out and locked the door carefully. He started strolling inside the plot while waiting for the driver to return.

When the cab driver went to buy the water bottles, the SUV parked near the highway started following him.

Nihal was getting restless as the driver had not been back. He tried his number, but no one picked up. After about an hour, Nihal saw the cab coming. By that time, Nihal had walked up to the highway. The driver said,

"Oh sir, I am sorry. I got a flat tire and had to change it. That took the time."

Nihal, was visibly angry. He sat down in the car and said to the driver,

"Ok, no problem, let's head back to Delhi."

"Sure, sir. Here is your water bottle."

The driver handed over the unopened water bottle to Nihal.

* * *

Both Samir and Dinesh reached Moti Nagar following the address on Google Maps. It was a crowded locality, so it took them time to find a parking spot and then walk back to the handloom shop. Dinesh went inside the shop and came immediately. Pratap's house was the third house on the lane behind the shop. Both entered the lane and found the house. As expected, the door was locked. It was around 12:30 pm. They would have to wait. Samir knew it would be long before Pratap would head home from work. They thought of going to their office and returning around 7 pm rather than waiting there.

* * *

Natasha was heading back from the seminar at FCCI. She was surprised at how persistently she sought an answer to her question. Both Swaminathan and Ameya had no answer. She wondered why there was no provision in the law that enabled citizens to disclose possession of foreign currency voluntarily. Let the authorities keep the money but there should be no penal action or prosecution. The citizen's voluntary disclosure of such currency would only add to the government's kitty, and the absence of such a provision compelled one to go to Hawala racketeers. It encouraged their business.

She suddenly remembered Neelesh. There was no call from him. Where was he? She called his number. Neelesh responded by saying,

"Hi, Natasha. Where have you been the whole day?"

Natasha laughed and said,

"I was going to ask the same question. Anyway, there was a seminar in FICCI today. I was one of the delegates. Archit asked me to attend it."

"So, you spent the whole day there?"

"Yeah. What about you?"

"I am at home. I had no case listed today. I preferred working from home."

"Ok. Tomorrow is a Sunday. What are the plans?"

"Nothing. Can we meet then?"

"Right, tomorrow morning we will talk and plan."

They disconnected. Kuku was listening. After a while, he asked.

"Was that Neelesh, sir?"

Natasha was looking at her emails on the phone. She continued checking and said,

"Yes. Why?"

"When I was at parking at FICCI, Kishan called. He said that Neelesh sir was not at home when he reported for duty, nor was his car there."

"Ok."

"Kishan was worried because Neelesh sir was not taking his calls either."

"Oh, Neelesh may be busy somewhere," she said.

But she wondered why Neelesh said he was at home all day, whereas as per Kishan, Neelesh was out. She said,

"Call Kishan and ask him whether sir is back or not."

Kuku spoke to Kishan for a while and said,

"No, madam. He is still not back."

Natasha wondered that for the last few days, Neelesh's behaviour was weird, and he lied to her. She shrugged her shoulders.

* * *

Ameya was sitting in her official car. She was used to speaking at seminars and events organized by different forums, chambers and associations. The seminar at FICCI was one such routine affair, with the only exception of the question by Natasha. She had answered tricky questions at different places. She was used to this. She was known in the department for putting forth her opinions and she was part of the draft committee, which had prepared the FEMA law.

She did not think that Natasha's question was just out of curiosity. Such questions arise during discussions, for which there is no answer as per law, but that day, the question by Natasha was not an innocent query. Ameya had never seen any delegate asking questions in such an emotional manner. Natasha seemed to be literally charged. The last two words uttered by Natasha, "HOW UNFORUNATE," kept echoing in Ameya's mind. The question was, no doubt, a valid question.

Ameya was thinking about the same. Natasha jumped from ten thousand dollars to a million dollars, as if it had practically happened to her or somebody close to her. Ameya realized that Natasha was desperate to know the lawful solution, and Natasha was correct that no parallel could be drawn between Income Tax Law and FEMA law. In income tax, one can always declare the income from 'other' sources and pay the tax. The Income Tax department often announces voluntary disclosure schemes to bring more citizens into the taxpayer net.

But FEMA law was different. Ameya had not taken much interest in the case of Nihal Singh being investigated. To her, the information appeared bogus from day one. On her own, she had never made queries from Raghunath regarding the case's progress. Raghunath, however, kept on briefing Ameya from time to time. She recollected that only the day before, Raghunath told her about a person coming out of the departure hall with two suitcases. He said that Samir and Dinesh are working on identifying that person.

All of a sudden, it occurred to her that Nihal was only a pawn in the game. What about Mulliani, the actual operator? More importantly, who had hired them for this transfer? Who was Mulliani's client? She looked at her phone and called Raghunath,

"Good evening, madam," Raghunath received the call on the other end.

"Yeah, good evening. Raghunath, what is the update?"

"Update?"

"On Nihal Singh's case?"

It came as a pleasant surprise to Raghunath. For the first time, Ameya had asked that question. He said,

"Madam, we are looking for the other person who came from the airport departure gate. His name is Pratap. We have got his name, telephone number and address. Samir and Dinesh are already on the job to bring Pratap for interrogation."

"Ok. Just tell me one thing. Have you ever checked the call details of Mulliani?"

"Yes, we checked the call details for the day of arrest and immediately after that, Mulliani switched off the phone."

"What about earlier call details?"

"Earlier meaning?"

"Raghunath, somebody must have given him the money. Can we not trace out that person? He must have given him Indian currency in cash and …"

"No. No madam. My informer has told me that Mulliani was handed over hard currency in US dollars only."

"It's a big amount. The person must have bought dollars from the grey market. The exchange of such a huge amount cannot go unnoticed. What are we doing? Use your resources and find out who was looking for such a huge amount."

"I'll do that."

"And one more thing, check the call details of Mulliani for the last month. Some calls must be routine calls. Just see if there are any unusual calls. You know what I mean."

"Yes, madam."

"I want all the call details in an hour."

"Sure."

Raghunath disconnected the call and was surprised at Ameya's sudden interest in Nihal's case.

* * * * *

Chapter - XXIII

When the cab returned to Delhi, Nihal went to the money changer and got the $20,000 exchanged into Indian currency. Then he went to the friend from whom he had borrowed the money and returned it. After that, he called Vikram.

"Sir, good evening," Nihal said.

"Yes, Nihal," Vikram replied.

"Sir, are you still in office?"

"No. It's already 7 pm. I am back at my home. Are you in the mood to pay the fees?"

"In fact, yes."

Vikram laughed and said,

"Who denies money? I am forwarding my address. Can you come?"

"Yes."

In another half an hour, Nihal was at Vikram's place. He gave him a packet.

"How much?" asked Vikram.

"Sir, you'll not be disappointed.

Vikram laughed and said,

"Mulliani must be annoyed. By now, he must have figured out that I helped you get your passport released from the ED office."

"No way, sir."

"Anyway, what are your plans?"

"Not decided yet, but I may travel in a day or two."

"Good. All the best."

Nihal's cab was waiting. He asked the driver to drop him at Moti Nagar, where he had picked him up. The driver, too, was tired. It was a hectic day for him but a good ride from his business point of view.

Nihal got down near the handloom shop in Moti Nagar. As he was about to enter the lane, he saw Pratap being escorted by Samir and Dinesh. Nihal quickly hid behind a truck and watched. Pratap was made to sit in a vehicle and all three drove off. He stood there and then cautiously moved towards Pratap's house. No one was there. The house was locked from the outside. Nihal had an extra key. He opened the door and went in. He switched on the light. Nothing seemed to have been disturbed.

Nihal was in shock; he sat down on a chair. His scheme was foolproof. How did the ED reach Pratap? And when they had taken Pratap away, they would find out where the suitcases were hidden. Going to Sampla again and bringing the suitcases to Pratap's house was also risky. He could only pray that Pratap would remain strong and not divulge the hideout. Nihal was trembling. Getting hold of Pratap meant the ED knew his involvement. It was only a matter of time. He had to keep his fingers crossed.

* * *

Ameya had reached home. She changed into casuals, went to the washroom, spent about five minutes and came out. There was a missed call on her phone from Raghunath. She called back.

"Yes?"

"Madam, Pratap has been picked up. Samir and Dinesh are reaching the office with him. I am also going to the office. We will see if we can extract some new information from him."

"What about Mulliani's call details?"

"I had got that checked for the last two months period. Most of the calls, both outgoing and incoming, are repetitive."

"You mean for the entire duration of two months?"

"Yes. But there is one number on which incoming or outgoing calls lasted three days before Nihal's interception. This number is not on the call before those three days."

"You mean, this is a new person contacting him?"

"It so appears. Shall I find out who the person is? I'll ask the system people."

"Please do."

They disconnected. In another 20 minutes, it was conveyed to Ameya the number belonged to Sukhdev.

After dinner, Ameya opened her laptop and typed Sukhdev on Facebook. There were more than 60 profiles listed in front of her. It was a futile exercise to go through all of them. She looked at Natasha's business card, closed Facebook and googled Sukhdev, Olympic Paints. She couldn't find anything relevant on page one so she clicked on the next tab. It was there and clicking it took her to his LinkedIn profile. Sukhdev's picture was as DGM of Olympic Paints. It appeared that Sukhdev had created his profile but was hardly active.

Ameya took a screenshot and started tapping the table and wondering whether the money belonged to Olympic Paints. She tried to make a sequence. Olympic Paints, perhaps, wanted to send money in US dollars outside India. The job was given to the CFO, Natasha, who further assigned the job to Sukhdev. Sukhdev had talked to Mulliani. Mulliani gave the money in two suitcases to Nihal, who embroiled Pratap, intending to cheat. The suitcases were exchanged at the airport and Pratap was offloaded as he came up with some excuse. Was that a proper sequence? She kept thinking but felt that there were gaps, some missing links. If it was the company's money, why did Natasha say, "Let us say it is a windfall." Natasha was more worried about the disposal of dollars. The money could not have belonged to her company. Money transfer, legally or illegally, was common among corporates. No one would talk about a "windfall" unless there was one. Then she also murmured, "How unfortunate."

She could only conclude that Sukhdev, Nihal and Pratap were the pawns, and Mulliani was the operator, but who was Mulliani's client – Olympic Paints. Natasha or someone else? But she had a gut feeling that Natasha had some connection with Nihal Singh's case, and if that was correct, how was she in the possession of three million dollars in cash? To the best of Ameya's experience, salaried individual couldn't have that kind of liquid cash.

She shut her laptop, closed her eyes and leaned on the back of her bed.

* * *

Neelesh got a call from the lawyer Vinod Goyal, who was handling the ALTARA brand name dispute.

"Good evening, sir," Vinod said.

"Oh yes, good evening." He looked at his watch. The time was 10:15 pm and wondered, why Vinod is calling at this hour?

"I am sorry for calling you so late."

He was polite and said, "Not at all. I normally go to bed at around 11 pm. What's the news?"

"Sir, I agree with your proposal. I have talked to my client. Cherry Hills. They have agreed that Suman Foundation shall be discouraged from filing another PIL or to appeal before the Supreme Court. My other client will withdraw his application for registration of the ALTARA brand. It will be done on Monday."

"Thank you, Vinod. I am obliged. I'll do the needful at my end."

"Good. It was a nice proposal."

"May I ask one thing? Just out of curiosity."

"Yes, please."

"Justice Chowdhary had an excellent reputation. How did you manage that? No other lawyer could dare to talk to him." Neelesh said on a clear presumption that Justice Chowdhary was the presiding judge on the bench.

Vinod kept quiet for a bit and finally said,

"I was called by Justice Chowdhary the next day after the hearing. The proposal came from his side."

"Oh God. He too."

"Yes. That was perhaps his first and last time. His only condition was that it should be in US dollars."

"And you did that?"

"Yes, so many money changers are sitting in the grey market. They charge a little extra money over and above the market rate to do the job for you."

Neelesh was listening. They chatted for some time and finally hung up.

* * *

Nihal had two options. Either to wait till the next day to see if Pratap held up to the two interrogators, Samir and Dinesh. Then, the money would be safe and could be moved from the hideout. The second option was to leave the country immediately and save himself. The recovery of the money would lead to the arrest of Pratap and Nihal. The second option was perhaps the only one. He was worried about Mulliani. Till now, he had saved himself but with the recent developments, Mulliani would catch up and find him.

He had to decide quickly. If the money at Sampla remained safe, it could be collected later.

* * *

Pratap was brought to the ED office. After having a light dinner, Samir started talking to Pratap. He said,

"Do you know why we have brought you here?"

"Yes, because Nihal is staying with me, and he was arrested, I know."

Samir looked at him with a serious face and said,

"You had exchanged two suitcases with Nihal at the airport and did not travel."

"Exchange? What exchange? I didn't travel, yes. That is there on record."

"Those suitcases were your suitcases?"

"Yes, sir."

"Where are those? These were not at your place. We had looked for suitcases at your place."

"It had my clothes. I emptied the suitcases and disposed of them. Those were old suitcases."

Samir looked at Dinesh and smiled. He said,

"Are you playing with us? How far have you studied?"

"Didn't finish school, sir," Pratap replied.

"Do you know what Nihal had said in the court?"

"No, sir."

"He didn't tell you?"

"Nihal told me that he was arrested for carrying ten thousand dollars and got bail the next day."

"He didn't tell you that there were three million dollars, which he was carrying. He said that in front of the magistrate."

"Three million dollars," said Pratap with his eyes wide open. Samir could see that it was news for Pratap. He seemed genuinely not aware of the bounty. Meanwhile, Raghunath too entered the room. He said,

"What's happening?"

"Beating around the bush. He is not telling us anything," Samir said.

"Nothing so far. But he will speak soon." Samir said while looking at Pratap sternly. Raghunath came out of the room and signalled to Samir. Samir followed him. Raghunath told him about his conversation with Ameya. He also said she wanted to find out who purchased the three million US dollars from the grey market. Samir was listening. Raghunath said,

"I will use my contacts. You can also check in with your contacts. According to her, such big buying could not go unnoticed."

"She is right. I'll start investigating tomorrow."

"Oh no, Samir. She wants the results by tomorrow."

Samir kept quiet for a few seconds and said,

"Sir, I'll do my best."

"Ok, you make this man talk. We have to find the money and this man knows where it is."

Raghunath went away.

* * * * *

Chapter - XXIV

It was a Sunday winter morning. Ameya looked outside. It was overcast. She got up and prepared a cup of tea and took it back to the bed. There was no hurry. She started sipping tea and also looked at her phone. There was yet to be a message from Raghunath. She was tempted to call Raghunath or Samir to know as to whether Pratap had confessed and what is the status of the recovery. But she preferred to wait. It was just 7:30 am.

She opened Facebook and searched Natasha Chowdhary. That was easy. The profile she was looking for was sitting right on top. She clicked on her profile picture. Natasha had posted a lot about herself: her education, experience, and previous and present jobs. There were a few pictures with her college friends. There was one picture with her father. The photo was recent. It appeared that her father had passed away recently, and there were comments from some of her friends and condolence messages. From these messages, Ameya could gather that Natasha's father was a retired Punjab and Haryana High Court judge.

Ameya closed Facebook and started looking at her e-mails while sipping her tea.

At about 9 am when Ameya was in the kitchen readying her breakfast, there was a ring on her phone. It was Raghunath.

"Good morning, madam,"

"Good morning,"

"Finally, madam, Pratap has confessed. Though he is not aware of the dollars, being there in the suitcases, he has told where the suitcases were kept."

"Where?"

"He says the suitcases are hidden in a location in Sampla. It's a village on the way to Rohtak. Both Nihal and Pratap belonged to Sampla."

"So, what's the plan?"

"I've called four IOs and asked Samir and Dinesh to go home. They needed rest. The four IOs will accompany Pratap, who will take them to the location where the money is hidden."

"How far is this place?" Ameya enquired.

"Maybe two hours from Delhi," Raghunath said.

"Ok, any update on who purchased the dollars from the grey market?"

"Yes, I am on the job. Samir has also contacted a couple of people dealing in foreign exchange. We hope to come up with something."

"I am at home, so keep me updated."

"Sure."

They disconnected. Ameya was back to preparing her breakfast.

* * *

Nihal was at the airport by 8:30 am. He decided it was best to leave Delhi for now and bought a ticket for Mumbai. The flight was scheduled for 10:05 am departure. He wanted to wait for a few more days. It was difficult to leave the money like that. He would take a chance, even if there was a slight possibility of getting the money back. And if the ED could lay their hands on those suitcases, he would fly to Bangkok or Hong Kong as getting a visa for both these countries is not difficult.

He preferred to stay in Mumbai and try to keep a tab on the case. He wanted to be where Mulliani and his men might not look for him.

* * *

Two IOs were in the front seat and the other two were in the rear seat. Pratap was made to sit on the rear seat between two IOs. They left the ED office at 10 am and hoped to reach Sampla by noon.

* * *

When Samir reached his home, Vidhi was awake, but she looked in a bad mood. Samir asked,

"What happened? Are you ok?"

Vidhi looked at him and said, "I think, I married the wrong person. You have not bothered to know about your wife, for last week."

Samir came forward and embraced her. He said,

"I am sorry but we are near the completion of an investigation."

"Then some other investigation will come up," Vidhi took a jibe.

"No, dear. I'll take leave for a couple of days and we will go on a vacation," Samir tried to appease his wife.

It didn't seem to cheer up Vidhi. Samir said,

"I'll take a bath. Could you give me something light to eat? I need some rest."

"Ok," said Vidhi and went towards the kitchen. Samir was thinking that Vidhi was making a genuine complaint. He was sure that once the recovery was made, his role would more or less come to an end.

He took a towel and went to the bathroom.

* * *

The flight for Mumbai left at 10:05 am, and Nihal was on it.

* * *

Natasha was at her Gurugram home. She had planned to visit her Dwarka home. She was not sure about whether she will be meeting Neelesh. She had asked Kuku to come. Generally, Sundays were off days for Kuku, but when required, Natasha would call him.

It was around 11am. Her phone rang. It was Archit.

"Good morning, sir,"

"Good morning. Hope I am not disturbing you on a Sunday?"

"No. Not at all, sir."

"How was the seminar yesterday?"

"Great, sir,"

"I heard you spoke well and got noticed among all the delegates."

"Oh, that. No sir, I put up a genuine question and ..."

"I know. I got a call from Swaminathan. He told me about your query and how you put it up."

"Swaminathan, sir, do you know him?"

"Yes. I met him long back, when my father was handling this business. Swaminathan was a friend of my father. I am not regularly in touch with him. He had all praises for you."

"Sir, I spoke extempore."

"But it was relevant."

"Yes, sir."

"Anyway, enjoy your Sunday. We will discuss more about this tomorrow."

"Thank you for calling, sir."

* * *

A person engaged in money exchange business must register with FEMA and RBI. Anyone can approach them and exchange currency for different countries. The money exchangers have to keep an account of the person coming to exchange, and there was also a rule that for exchange purposes, Indian currency only up to Rs. 50,000/- could be received in cash. If the customer wants to exchange more money, it must be routed through a banking channel.

However, most money changers used this registration as a façade and sold foreign exchange in the grey market. All such transactions were in cash and no official entries were made.

The ED people were aware of it. The small transactions in cash over and above Rs. 50,000/- were ignored. The money changers were aware of the same. Very few would take the risk of dealing in big cash. People, among those were usually in touch with the ED people and the ED staff used them as informants too. Raghunath had called one such money changer in the morning, but he didn't pick up. His name was Zameer Ahmed. Raghunath again called Zameer at about 11:30 am.

He asked, "Yes, Zameer. What's the news?"

"Nothing sir. I have talked to some people in the trade. No such big buying of US dollars has been noticed."

"Recently?"

"Yes, sir, not in last month."

"Can you go beyond one month? We are sure that such a big transaction has taken place. It could be beyond one month, six months or a year."

Zameer thought for a moment and said,

"Sir, while I was checking for three million dollars, as you had asked me to check, I heard that a customer was interested in buying that much cash in US dollars about seven or eight months back. Whether he got it or not could never be known because it would never flow from a single source. It is not possible."

"And who could be the person?"

"Sir, I didn't check that."

"Can you please try to find out? Though the transaction was made seven or eight months back it may not be relevant. I would like to know more."

Zameer said,

"Please hold on. I'll see if I can get that information."

Raghunath kept the phone on hold. After more than five minutes, Zameer was back online. He said,

"No sir, no one knows the name. One of the traders said he was perhaps a lawyer from Chandigarh."

"Ok. Thank you, Zameer. If I need anything further, I may call back."

"I will be happy to help, sir."

They disconnected. Raghunath called Ameya and told her about this conversation. Ameya thanked Raghunath.

*   *   *

Ameya felt an excitement; perhaps the puzzle had a solution. The missing piece had just come. About seven or eight months back, a lawyer from Chandigarh was looking for three million US dollars in the market.

Natasha's father retired around that time. It appeared the money was meant as a bribe. She had gathered that Justice Chowdhary was an honest and upright judge throughout his life. She also knew of instances, where judges had taken hefty bribes in deciding their last cases, even though they were dead honest throughout their careers.

If her presumptions were correct so far, Natasha was unaware of the money, and after her father's death, she had uncovered the cash at her father's house. She is an educated woman, and would have explored all possibilities to dispose of the money legally. She could not have kept that money at home any longer. Finally, she would have decided to send it out through an operator and contacted Mulliani.

Ameya laughed out loud. She seemed to have solved the mystery and now knew who Mulliani's client was.

She would have to wait for the recovery. That would be the real material evidence.

*   *   *   *   *

Chapter - XXV

Pratap pointed towards the stone crusher from the highway. The car turned left and reached the compound's entrance, which had a brick wall on all four sides. They all exited the car and Pratap led them towards the room. To his surprise, there was no lock on the door. It was latched from the outside. Jatin, who was one of the IOs, asked,

"What happened?"

"Sir, the door is not locked." Pratap immediately opened the latch and pushed the door. They all entered.

A bedsheet was lying on the cot. Pratap looked under the cot. **The suitcases were missing.** He started trembling. Jatin said,

"Yes, where are the suitcases?"

"Sir, I left them under the cot. But they are not here now."

Jatin pulled him up from a sitting position by his collar and said,

"Stop making a fool of us. You brought us all the way to show this site and to tell us the suitcases are not here."

Pratap folded his hands. There were tears in his eyes. He said,

"Sir, I am telling the truth. I kept them here."

The IOs were looking at each other. They were disappointed. One of them even punched Pratap in frustration. Pratap sat down on the floor and started crying.

"Sir, they were here, yesterday. Nihal had come here to get some money out of the suitcases. But he was not to shift or take away the suitcases. Sir, believe me. I am telling you the truth."

"No, you are not telling us the truth," said Jatin.

"Sir, believe me."

"Only you and Nihal knew about this place. If you are telling the truth, Nihal has taken away both the suitcases."

"But that was not in the plan."

Jatin looked at him and said,

"Have you both not talked to each other since yesterday?"

"Once, when he was coming back from this place. Nihal had called me and told me that he would be coming home late as he was to settle some accounts."

"Was he sounding worried?"

"No."

"And?"

"That's all, sir. You picked me up before he came back."

Jatin handed him his phone and said,

"Call him."

"Sir, where is my phone?" He may not pick up seeing a new number."

"Your phone is at the office. Anyway, call Nihal from my phone."

Pratap called. Nihal's phone was switched off. Jatin took the phone from him and tried the number again. It was switched off.

Jatin went out of the room and came out of the compound. He called Raghunath.

"Sir, good afternoon."

"Yes, what happened?"

"The suitcases are not here. We are at a factory in Sampla, where Pratap claimed he hid the two suitcases."

"He must be making a fool of us."

"Maybe, but, it appears that whatever he is saying is true. Nihal had visited his site yesterday. He told Pratap that he would take some money from the suitcases to settle few accounts."

Raghunath was disappointed. The money had disappeared, yet again. Jatin said,

"Sir."

"Yes, I am listening. Will it be worthwhile to send someone to Pratap's place? Nihal might be there. Money might be there?"

"Let me see. You may all come back. Bring Pratap with you."

Raghunath was deeply involved in the case from the beginning. It was his informant who had shared the tip. He was expecting some positive information from the IOs and he was waiting to tell that to Ameya. She had also developed a keen interest in the case now. To tell her that nothing has been found would again be embarrassing. First, he decided to call Samir.

"Hello, Samir."

Samir, who had just woken up, said.

"Yes, sir."

"Were you sleeping? I am sorry, but it is important."

"What, sir?"

"Nothing has been found at the hideout where Pratap had led the team. I just got a call from Jatin."

"Oh God," said Samir in desperation. He said, "Now, what do we do, sir?"

"You have to visit Pratap's house to find out whether Nihal returned after the team left with Pratap. You may take Dinesh along with you."

"Sir, I'll go, but do you expect we will find something there?"

"No. I do not expect, let's take a chance. If Nihal is there, bring him to the office. I want to confront both Pratap and Nihal."

"Ok, sir."

They disconnected. Raghunath called Ameya,

"Good afternoon, madam."

"Yes, any update?"

"Nothing has been found where Pratap claims he left the two suitcases."

Ameya kept quiet for a few moments. Then said,

"Ok, tell me in detail."

Raghunath narrated the conversation he had with Jatin and also that he had asked Samir to visit Pratap's house immediately. Ameya kept listening and finally said,

"Something is wrong somewhere. *I fail to understand the failure.*"

She disconnected the call. Raghunath kept thinking. Ameya was annoyed. The department had to submit a report to the magistrate. The recovery of the US dollars would have saved their embarrassing position. Where had they gone wrong?

* * *

When there was a bell, Natasha was getting ready to go to her Dwarka home. She opened the door. It was Kuku.

"Yes, Kuku."

"Madam, Kishan has come. He wants to talk to you."

"Why? What happened?"

"He says Neelesh sir has fired him from the job."

"Fired?"

"Neelesh sir had asked Kishan not to come from tomorrow. He is upset and has come to request you for some other job."

"Ok. Send him upstairs and you take out the car. We are leaving."

"I'll send him."

In another five minutes, Kishan was standing before her.

"Yes, Kishan, what happened?"

"Madam, can you get me a job somewhere else," said Kishan with folded hands.

"What have you done to annoy Neelesh?"

"Nothing, madam. It was sudden. Yesterday, I kept waiting. Neelesh sir came late in the evening. I was there. He called me and gave me the salary for this month. He asked me not to report for duty from Monday onwards."

Natasha kept thinking. Kishan was sad. His eyes were moistened. She brought a glass of water for him and kept talking. Finally, she assured him that she would try to find a job for him.

*　*　*

In another hour, Samir reported that Pratap's house is locked. No one was seen there. Raghunath asked them to come back. There was no point in unnecessarily waiting there. Nihal would have moved himself to some other place.

The only other person who knew about the latest developments is Mulliani. He thought of meeting Mulliani, but then it occurred to him to first talk to his informer, Topaz. There is a big parking lot opposite the Supreme Court of India. It is difficult to find a parking spot there during the week, but since it was Sunday, getting parking was not a hassle. Raghunath parked his car at one corner. He didn't have to wait for long. The front door opened; Topaz sat down alongside Raghunath. They smiled at each other. Raghunath told him about the follow-up action and nabbing of Pratap, hoping they might be able to lay hands on three million dollars. Raghunath said,

"Can you tell me?"

"What about the money?" Topaz asked.

"Yes, It's the second failure."

Topaz looked at Raghunath sympathetically and said,

"Sir, I gave you the information at the first instance. That was true in all respects. What Nihal and Pratap did was not known to me. This story of the suitcases getting swapped at the airport is news to me. So, how can I tell you about what happened to the money?

Raghunath knew that Topaz had never spoken to him in this tone. Topaz, too, was not happy with the developments. An informer gives the information for two reasons – either to cause damage to the other party or to expect a cash reward in exchange for the information. Such cash rewards depend upon the amount recovered. No recovery means no reward. Topaz was aware of that. Raghunath was an Assistant Director with the ED. Topaz said,

"Sir, I am sorry for being rude."

"It's ok. Whatever you said is correct. I somehow presumed that you may know about Pratap, too."

"No sir, I know nothing about Nihal swapping the suitcases. And I am also sure that Mulliani had no idea about Nihal's sneaky plan."

"Look, we are certain the suitcases were swapped at the airport. We have the evidence. Pratap has confessed it. I wonder if the plan to exchange suitcases was known to only two people, Nihal and Pratap. Can there be a third person who was aware?"

Topaz looked at Raghunath straight in his eyes and said,

"Are you hinting at Mulliani?" He continued,

"No, had Mulliani come to know about this, I am sure he must have taken some drastic step."

"Like?"

"Like, you know. You are well aware. Nihal would have been punished for his transgression."

Topaz looked purposely at Raghunath and smiled. Raghunath could see that Topaz could tell something. Raghunath said slowly,

"Do you want to share something?"

"Do I? Sir, if I ask the same question."

"I didn't get you. What are you pointing at?"

"Sir, did you meet Mulliani?"

Raghunath was in shock. The meeting with Mulliani was discreet. It was not to be disclosed. He kept quiet. Topaz said,

"Sir, you had met Mulliani and perhaps talked to him."

"How do you know?"

"Sir, there is nothing to worry about. You need not burden yourself by thinking about how I came to know about the meeting. There are more than a hundred operators in the city. You must have got the profiles of most of them. Out of those, only six or seven operators are top players. Their network communication system and secrecy are infallible. Things are shared among them but never go out. Your meeting with Mulliani was known to these top players."

"But it doesn't go out? How do you know?"

"Sir, you told Mulliani about baggage tags recovered from Nihal's house. You told him the brand also. That much information was sufficient for Mulliani to infer what would have happened. You wanted to know from me who could be the third person. Sir, you gave the clue to Mulliani. Do I need to say more?"

Raghunath was looking like a fool. How could he have made such a blunder! Ameya was right when she said, "Something is wrong somewhere." Topaz said,

"Sir. I am again sorry that I am speaking too much, but I think it was necessary to tell you because I may not meet you again in future."

"Why?"

"You have just asked me how I know about your meeting with Mulliani." He stopped for a while and opened the door of the car. He said,

"Sir, have you even realized I could be one of those six-seven people? The day you met Mulliani, you closed the door on me."

Topaz closed the door of the car and briskly walked away.

Raghunath placed his head on the steering wheel in desperation. The information was correct, and it was mishandled. No further hope was left.

* * * * *

Chapter - XXVI

Natasha went to her Dwarka flat to bring back a few things. She put those in a bag. Then, she called the domestic helper to clean the house. She was in Dwarka for about two hours already. However, she was still waiting to get a call from Neelesh for a meeting. When she got free, she called Neelesh.

"Hello, what happened? We were to meet today."

"Oh, I was just about to call."

"Where are you?"

"At home."

"Ok. I am coming to your home. From there we'll go together. Have you had your lunch?"

"No."

"I have also not eaten. It's already late, but we will find a good place to go."

"Hey, don't worry. There are a lot of places around my home. Call me when you are downstairs and I'll come."

"Sure."

They disconnected. Natasha took the bag and came down. She asked Kuku to keep the bag at the back of the car, and they headed to Neelesh's house.

From Dwarka to Vasant Kunj, it's a half an hour drive. She didn't remember Neelesh's address but knew the location well. She had been to his house a few times. She asked Kuku,

"Do you know, Neelesh, Sir's house?"

"Yes, madam."

"How far is it now?"

"About to reach."

"Park the car, and we'll be back soon."

"Right, madam."

Kuku took a left turn from under a flyover. The first gate on the left side belonged to Neelesh's apartment complex. Kuku parked the car. Natasha climbed the stairs and rang the bell.

"Oh, you are here. Please come inside." Neelesh said as he opened the door. He continued,

"I told you to give me a call. You took the trouble to climb the stairs."

"Still young enough to climb the stairs."

Natasha smiled at him, Neelesh kissed her on the cheek and said,

"You'll always remain young and beautiful."

"Now, what is the plan? Where are we going?"

"Do you want a quick bite or prefer a formal place?"

"It's your choice where you want to take me."

Both laughed. Neelesh said,

"We can go to Hyatt. It's not very close, but I am sure you'll enjoy it."

Neelesh got up. Natasha said,

"I got to use the washroom."

"Oh sure," Neelesh directed her towards the bedroom. After a few minutes, she was back. Together, they got down.

* * *

Nihal had reached Mumbai. He checked in at a budget hotel near the airport at Vile Parle. He switched on his phone and saw the missed calls from an unknown number in the message box. Nihal wondered what happened to Pratap.

Pratap was brought back to the ED office. From there, he was taken to his house, got it opened and it was searched. Nothing was found, as was expected. Pratap was brought back to the ED office.

* * *

Neelesh and Natasha settled down at the coffee shop in Hyatt. It's a twenty-four-hour restaurant. Light snacks, combos, beverages, salads, etc., were available anytime. The restaurant had a lunch buffet, but it was over by the time they reached.

Natasha ordered a vegetable sandwich with potato wedges. Neelesh asked for a combo of rice with a vegetable and curry. Once the food was served, Natasha said,

"Where were you yesterday?"

"I told you; I was at home. Why are you getting inquisitive?"

She laughed and said,

"You had asked Kishan not to come for work from tomorrow onwards."

"Did he tell you?"

"Kuku was telling me."

"Oh."

"Was he not good driver?"

"Natasha, we are not here to discuss about a driver."

"Yes, of course not. It just occurred to me and I asked."

Neelesh kept eating with a spoon. After a while, he said,

"I am going to Singapore."

"When?"

"Tomorrow."

"And you are telling me now?"

Natasha said with eyes wide open.

"It was sudden. You know my brother is settled there. I had told you."

"Perhaps, yes."

"My mother is staying with him. She is not keeping well and insisted I visit her."

"And for how long will you be staying there?"

"The initial plan is for two months, but it depends on her health."

Natasha took a bite of a sandwich and said,

"You would have gone without telling me but for this meeting. It's not fair."

Neelesh smiled and said,

"How can you think that I will leave without informing you? You see, I will have to stay away from you for two months."

"Or maybe more."

Neelesh shrugged. Natasha asked,

"Who will be handling your work here in your absence?"

"Two of my juniors are there. They are quite competent. I am sure they will be able to handle the routine work. They would seek adjournments for tricky matters. Otherwise, I will always be available on the internet and video."

"That's right. You can make some arrangements, but employees like us cannot go on long leave."

Neelesh just smiled. They kept sitting and talking for about one and a half hours. Finally, Neelesh settled the cheque and they got up to leave. As they were coming out, Natasha asked him,

"At what time is your flight tomorrow?"

"It's at 5:30 pm."

Natasha thought for a moment and said,

"Ok, I'll come to your place and pick you up. Let us meet for one last time before you go."

"Oh dear, why do you say last time?"

Natasha laughed and said,

"At what time do you intend to leave your place? Around 3 pm?"

"Yes, but I will be able to manage on my own. The airport is not far from Vasant Kunj."

"I know, I know. It is just so that I can spend a little more time with you. In any case, you are not coming back for at least two months."

"Ok, as you say."

"I'll come at around 2 pm. I will buy some food on my way. We'll have lunch together and then leave for the airport."

Both came out holding each other's hand. Natasha called Kuku and asked him to be at the entrance of the Hyatt.

*　*　*

After dropping Neelesh at his residence, Natasha called Sukhdev while sitting in the car.

"Yes, madam," it said Sukhdev.

"Where are you?"

"At my home."

"Can you come to my place in Gurugram?"

"Anything urgent?"

"Yes and no. If it is not convenient …"

"I'll come, madam. At what time shall I come?"

"I'll be reaching home in the next hour. Any time after that."

"Ok."

Natasha told Kuku that she had to go to Vasant Kunj Mall. It was not far off from Neelesh's residence.

*　*　*

Ameya saw that there were two missed calls from Raghunath. She had lost all interest in the case. Without recovering the money, the case was worthless. She called Raghunath.

"Yes,"

"Madam, nothing has been recovered from Pratap's house."

"So. Why are you telling me?"

Raghunath asked hesitantly,

"Shall we allow Pratap to go? We cannot detain him for more than twenty-four hours. Or, if…"

"Allow him to go and please don't call me again. We'll discuss the issue in the office tomorrow morning. Is that understood?"

"Yes, madam."

Ameya slammed the phone down. She was upset that her team was not as efficient as they should be to deserve a place in an investigating agency like the ED.

*　*　*

Pratap was back home. He was disgusted and was in a bad mood. He should not have trusted Nihal. In a fit of anger, he called Nihal. The phone rang this time, but no one received the call. After ten minutes, there was a call on Pratap's phone. It was from a landline phone. He picked up,

"Pratap," It was Nihal.

"Nihal, do you know because of you I was picked up by the ED? I was beaten and I had to tell them where the suitcases were kept."

"Please don't be angry. Have they recovered the money?"

"Recovered? Don't try to fool me. You went there yesterday. You picked up the suitcases and …"

"What are you saying? I picked up the suitcases. You mean …."

"Yes, the suitcases are not there. I had accompanied them to Sampla. There was no lock on the door. You took away the suitcases and the money, and I got harassed unnecessarily. They kept doubting that I had taken them to some wrong place."

"Pratap, my friend, I took some money and left the suitcases properly covered with the bedsheet. I locked the door of the room."

"Only you and me knew about it."

"Yes."

"Then how did they go missing? I have just reached home. I was detained the whole night."

"Pratap, let me think it through. It might be Mulliani. Though I doubt that but there is no possibility of any other person to have known."

"You mean somebody, after you left Sampla, would have taken the suitcases?"

"Yes"

"That means someone was possibly following you."

Nihal thought for a while and said,

"Yes, which means someone was keeping an eye on your house."

"Where are you?"

"I've come to Mumbai. Yesterday, I saw the ED staff escorting you out of your home when I was about to reach. I wanted to be away, particularly if it was Mulliani behind all this. I cannot face them again."

"You, please come back."

"I'll, but you need not worry. When no money was recovered, no one will come to you. I am worried about Mulliani. He definitely will be looking out for me."

Nihal kept assuring him and finally switched off the phone. He was wondering who could have followed him. Either it was one of Mulliani's men or could it be someone from the ED. But, again, whosoever it was, the money was gone. His complete plan was deflated. His only option now was to leave India.

* * * * *

Chapter - XXVII

The following day, Ameya called both Raghunath and Samir. They entered her room. They were both tensed. Ameya looked at them and signalled them to sit down. She noticed both were so scared that they forgot to say the customary good morning. She, however, smiled and said,

"Good morning."

They realized the slip and said,

"Very good morning, madam."

"Why are both of you looking so tense? You have done your job, sincerely. The results were not favourable."

"Madam, the result at the end that matters," Raghunath responded.

"Now, forget the case. Close the file; no more investigation. There are other things to be done. Concentrate on new leads. The world doesn't come to an end with one unsolved case."

Both men remained silent. She continued,

"Now cheer up. I'll handle the DG. You prepare a draft report to be submitted to the magistrate. Take the help of Krishnan, our PP. You know how to do it."

"Yes, madam," Raghunath said.

"Consult Krishnan. Tell him everything that we have tried. Don't omit anything. Before filing the report, show it to me. I will get it approved and signed by the DG."

"Yes, madam."

"That's all. You may leave now," she said, spreading her arms on the table.

Both Raghunath and Samir came out. They looked at each other. They had not expected such a discouraging end. They had solved a number of cases together and successfully but…

* * *

Natasha attended the meeting with Archit in the morning. She told him that she had rechecked last quarter's figures, and there were no discrepancies. They discussed the marketing strategy. Though it was not Natasha's domain of expertise, Archit often consulted non-marketing employees, too. When Natasha was to end the meeting, she said,

"Sir, I may leave around lunchtime."

"You mean you are not available post lunch?"

"Yes, sir. I've got to drop a friend at the airport."

"Neelesh?" Archit asked.

That Natasha and Neelesh were on friendly terms was not a secret.

"Yes, sir," she said, smilingly.

"Is he going out of India?"

"Yes, sir, his mother is not well. She is in Singapore."

"Ok. Take care."

"Thank you, sir."

She came out of his cabin.

At 1:30 pm, she came out of the office and told Kuku that they would head to Neelesh's house and stop at a pizza parlour. At 2:10 pm she was at Neelesh's house, holding two pizza boxes. Neelesh opened the door. He looked at her and the pizza boxes. He came forward, embraced her and said,

"How lucky I am!"

"Still, you are going. Leaving me alone."

"Don't worry. We'll be in touch; I'll try to come as soon as possible."

They opened the boxes and started eating their respective pizzas while talking. Exactly, at 3 pm, they were ready to leave for the airport. Natasha said,

"Your luggage?"

"Yes. There are two suitcases and one laptop bag."

Natasha called Kuku upstairs and asked him to take the two suitcases and keep it at the back of the car. After that, Neelesh locked the door and both came down. They saw Kuku putting the suitcases in the boot of the vehicle and both sat down in the rear seat. Kuku was told to drive them to the airport's terminal 3. He started driving. Natasha and Neelesh kept talking, laughing and chiding each other. Kuku went into the lane heading towards the departure. He looked for an appropriate slot. As he stopped, Natasha said,

"Kuku, can you go, bring the trolley?" she pointed towards the site, where trollies were lined up. Neelesh opened the door to get down. Natasha put her arms around his neck and kissed him passionately. The fragrance of her body made him mad. For a few minutes, they were like that. From the corner of his eyes, Kuku was looking at them, holding the trolley loaded with two suitcases. When they both got down, Neelesh took hold of the trolley and smiled at Natasha. He took out his wallet and handed over Rs 500 to Kuku as a gesture. Natasha was looking. Finally, they bid farewell to each other. She kept standing there, looking at Neelesh walking towards the entrance. At the entrance, Neelesh looked up. They waved to each other and Neelesh went in.

Natasha sat in the car and asked Kuku to go to J W Marriot. It was just a ten-minute drive.

She got down at the entrance of J W Marriot and said to Kuku,

"I'll call you when I am ready to leave."

"Right, madam."

She went inside the hotel and walked straight to the end. On the left side was a twenty-four-hour restaurant K.3. She had also been to that place earlier. She put her purse on the table and sat down on a sofa. The time was around 3:35 pm. The eatery was not at all crowded at that time. Around six people were sitting in the corner, as if some conference was going on. A couple occupied two tables. A waiter came and placed the menu card on the table before Natasha. She didn't look at the menu card and said,

"Wine, white wine."

"Which one do you prefer, madam?"

The waiter asked and opened the page showing the list of wines. She just glanced at it and said,

"This one, Tall Horse."

"Anything else to...?"

"No, just Tall Horse."

A sparkling glass filled with Tall Horse was placed before her, within 10 minutes. Natasha was looking at her phone. She messaged Neelesh, "Let me know when you have boarded."

The reply came immediately, "Oh yes, check-in done. I am at the immigration counter."

"That's good," Natasha disconnected and smiled a mysterious smile. She picked up the glass and took a big sip. She kept the wine in her mouth for some time before gulping it. She was enjoying it. She had always preferred sitting alone like this. She was not in a hurry. She was taking the wine slowly, and when she finished it, she looked at the watch. The time was 4:40 pm. Neelesh's flight was scheduled for 5:30 pm. Boarding must have started or may start perhaps in another 10 – 15 minutes. She would get the message. She signalled to the waiter and asked him to repeat the drink. The waiter nodded and went away. After a while, when the waiter placed another glass of wine on the table before her, she heard a beep. It was Neelesh.

The message said, "Boarded."

"Good. Have a nice and safe journey," Natasha texted.

"Thank you," the prompt response came from Neelesh.

* * *

Natasha had booked a ticket for Dubai the same day. No one knew about her trip. Her flight was scheduled for 8:45 pm. She wanted to be at the airport before 6 pm. She was sipping the Tall Horse and was thinking, what to do. By the time she finished the second drink, she had arrived at a final decision. She quickly made the payment and called Kuku to come to the gate.

When she sat down in the car, she told Kuku to go to the departure terminal 3 of the airport. When the car stopped outside the departure hall, Kuku came out, brought a trolley and loaded two suitcases on the trolley. Natasha got down and handed over one thousand rupees to Kuku and said,

"I'll call you when I am back. Probably I am coming tomorrow night."

Kuku took the money, bowed, and sat back in the car. Natasha went inside the departure hall. The check-in counters for her flight were at Row A/B. She looked at the watch. It was 5.55pm. She went to help counter and spoke to them. The girl at the help counter was pointing towards the right corner.

* * *

Ameya was about to leave the office when there was a ring on her mobile phone. It was some landline number. She thought it might be a wrong number. But again, there was a ring from the same number. Normally, the mobile numbers of top bureaucrats were not easily available. She again disconnected. She called the peon and told him to ask the driver to bring the car near the gate. The peon left the room. As she was leaving her room, again, there was a ring from the same number. This time, she pressed the green sign.

"Yes, who is it?"

"Is it Joint Director, ED?"

"Who are you?" she asked in anger.

"Are you the Joint Director?" The person at the other end insisted.

"Yes."

"Listen carefully. At the departure hall opposite row A/B, there are washrooms for men and women. On a trolley...."

"From where did you get my number?"

Suddenly Ameya smiled and said,

"Yes, what were you saying?"

"A trolley is there near the washrooms. Two blue suitcases are placed on the trolley. It has the three million dollars you have been looking for. Send your team quickly before…"

"Before?"

"Before it is too late."

The person at the other end disconnected the call. Ameya went back to her table and called Raghunath. She told him about the anonymous caller and said,

"Go quickly, the suitcases are there. Take Samir and other IOs. At least four persons should be there in the team."

"What about the passenger?"

"Forget about the passenger. The first step is to rush to the airport and take possession of the suitcases and remember to take witnesses along with you. You have to make a seizure there only."

Raghunath was puzzled. 'Make a seizure' were the words which sounded like she had confirmed information.

* * *

At 6:45 pm, a team of ED officers reached the departure hall. Raghunath saw a trolley near the washrooms. There were two blue suitcases loaded on it. Raghunath and Samir looked around. The hall was crowded, full of passengers. Samir moved the trolley slightly, but no one came forward to claim them. They kept standing there for 7-8 minutes. Finally, Raghunath said,

"Let us take it to the customs room, located at the departure hall. A customs officer was sitting in uniform. Raghunath introduced himself and showed his identity card. Samir brought the trolley into the room and looked at Raghunath,

"So?"

"Open it. We have to make a seizure here."

Samir smiled and said,

"We have not even seen the money."

"I say open it. Break the locks."

One of the IOs sat down and started working on the locks. In another 15 minutes, the suitcases were open. On removing a few clothes, there were bundles of US dollars in denomination of 100 US dollars each. They counted. The amount worked out US $ 2,980,000. Samir said,

"Sir, it is twenty thousand less than three million."

"Please count again. It must be three million."

They counted again it was 2.98 million US dollars. All of them were excited. It was a big case. Raghunath came out and called Ameya,

"Yes, Raghunath. Have you got it?"

"Yeah, it is 2.98 million US dollars. Not exactly three million."

"No problem. Make a seizure."

"Madam, is there no information about the passenger?"

"Make an unclaimed seizure. And convey my congratulations to your team. Well done."

Raghunath was surprised that Ameya was so sure about the recovery this time. That was great. He came back into the room and said,

"I have conveyed to madam. There is no information about the passenger. We have to make an unclaimed seizure."

"Unclaimed?" Samir said.

"Yes, what is the problem?"

"No, not at all. Sir, it will take about one hour to prepare the documents."

"Take your time."

* * *

Natasha went to the counter where passengers with no checked-in bags were checking in. She was holding only her purse. The girl at the counter scanned her passport and handed the boarding pass. The time was 7:35 pm. She passed the immigration and security checks and reached the boarding gate at 7:55 pm. The boarding was scheduled to start at 8:15 pm. She sat down, closed her eyes and relaxed. There was a smile on her face. Suddenly, she remembered the next day was a working day. She had to inform Archit and find a plausible explanation for her absence from the office.

Natasha's flight was on time and took off exactly at 8:45 pm for Dubai.

* * * * *

Chapter - XXVIII

The day after the seizure, Ameya called Raghunath and Samir to her office. She smiled at them and said,

"Mission fulfilled?"

"Yes, madam, your information was perfect," Raghunath said.

"It started with your information, and I was not very happy then," Ameya said.

"Madam, the only regret will be that we have been unable to pinpoint the accused in this case. The seizure has been made unclaimed. Somebody left the trolley with suitcases at the departure hall."

"Yes, of course, but has it even occurred to you people the person carrying it inside might be the person who informed us."

"Who informed you, madam?" asked Raghunath. She smiled and said,

"I can have an informer too."

"So, you know the person?"

Ameya looked at them and said,

"I am simply saying that the person carrying the suitcases inside the departure hall could perhaps be the only person to inform."

Samir was listening to the conversation silently. He said,

"It is perhaps the same money taken away from the hideout."

"It is the same money," said Ameya stressfully.

"Twenty thousand dollars are less."

"Yeah, this is probably because Nihal had visited the place and taken out some money."

Ameya looked at Raghunath and said,

"Now you can prepare your investigation report with full confidence, which is to be submitted to the magistrate."

"Oh yes. That is not a problem now,"

"I've already briefed the DG and he was quite happy."

Soon, tea was served to all of them and they chatted over it.

* * *

When Raghunath and Samir came out of the room, Raghunath said,

"It appears Ameya madam knows the person who told her."

"Sir, you are probably right, but you know your informer. One has to cultivate the informers. She might have been doing this silently."

Raghunath patted Samir's shoulders and said,

"You are right."

They went in their respective rooms.

Mulliani heard whispers that the ED had made a seizure last night at the airport, but the information regarding the total amount recovered was not known. He thought it was a matter of time and that things would come out. He also gathered that Nihal had left the country without the money.

Natasha came back from Dubai late at night. Kuku was already at the airport to receive him. She went to her Dwarka house. She had a good night's sleep after a long time. The last couple of months were quite stressful, but finally, it's all over.

* * * *

Chapter - XXIX

Epilogue

Six months passed since Natasha's last trip to Dubai. Natasha had not met or spoken with Neelesh. Nor had Neelesh called her. It was a clean break-up.

Archit presented Natasha with an IHC membership card. The India Habitat Centre (IHC) at Lodhi Road is quite an elite institution, and getting their membership is tough. The IHC has a provision to offer institutional memberships. This membership was for two years. Natasha had been there a couple of times. It was undoubtedly a prestigious institute. They have a Pan Asian restaurant on the sixth floor, accessible only to the members. She preferred to go alone. It was summer month, perhaps June. She visited the restaurant for lunch one of the Saturdays. As she entered, the staff escorted her to a table. At one of the corners, there was a window overlooking the view outside. At the centre table, about 12-13 ladies were having lunch and talking. Natasha had noticed that most of these ladies were either the wives of top bureaucrats or they were bureaucrats. On the table in front of her were a few people. Perhaps they were colleagues working together and were in the age group of 35-45 years.

She asked for white wine and some spring rolls. It was served to her within 15 minutes. The spring rolls were delicious. She took a sip from the wine glass and was looking at the plate of spring rolls served with dips when she heard a voice,

"Good afternoon, Natasha."

Natasha looked up. It was Ameya. It took Natasha a few moments to recognize her. She stood up smilingly and extended her hand.

"Good afternoon, madam."

They shook hands. Ameya asked,

"Are you waiting for someone, or are you enjoying alone?"

"No, no one is joining me today. Please sit."

"I hope I am not disturbing you, Natasha."

"Not at all, madam. What'll you have?"

Ameya smiled at her and said,

"Drop the 'madam,' please. Call me Ameya."

"Oh, you are the Joint Director of the ED. To call you by your first name will be against protocols."

"We can be good friends."

"Of course, madam, Ameya."

"That's better, and I'll not have anything. I was sitting with that group of ladies. They have finished. I saw you sitting here alone and walked up."

"Still." She signalled to the waiter and asked for one more glass of wine.

Ameya said,

"Thank you for your information about the US dollars lying in the departure hall."

Natasha looked at her with eyes wide open. Ameya said,

"Come on, we are friends. I recognized your voice that day on the telephone. I researched when you asked about declaring or disposing of foreign currency at the FICCI seminar. We are skillful enough. The emotions in your query were not professional. Those were personal."

Natasha was thinking about whether the meeting was contrived. She said,

"No. Ameya. I never called you to give any information. There is perhaps some misunderstanding."

Ameya replied, "Natasha. I am not talking to you as the Joint Director. As a true citizen, I am thankful that you, offered your money for seizure. And don't worry, the case has long been closed, and I have recommended to the ministry to make provisions for the situation that you had asked about."

Natasha was still quiet. She took the glass of wine, had a sip and said,

"Anyway, Ameya, that matter is closed, right? There is no point in discussing it further."

"I can see that you are not trusting me. I am confirming the matter has ended and assure you that there is no need to be afraid. You can share anything with me."

Natasha smiled and said,

"You said you recognized my voice. So, that means I shared the most important information with you. What else is left?"

"See, I am curious to know how you got back that money. Was it you who stole the suitcases from the hideout? The more I think, the stronger my belief gets that you cannot go to that extent, looking at your background."

Natasha looked around. Most of the tables were now unoccupied. She asked for one more drink. Ameya, however, denied any further drink. She was yet to finish the first one. She still kept quiet. Ameya could see that Natasha was not ready to open. She said,

"After your father's death, you found those three million US dollars from his house and you were shocked. You didn't know what to do. You took the help of Mulliani to transfer the money to Dubai, which failed. That failure was because Mulliani's man defrauded him. Our case also became a laughing joke. This much I could figure out. I will say it was stage one."

Natasha realized that Ameya knew too much. Ameya continued.

"Your query at the FICCI seminar was a very specific one. It piqued my interest and I inquired about the reason behind your query. Until then we were unaware of who Mulliani's client was. That it was you - Natasha Chowdhary- was the stage two."

Ameya looked at Natasha and said,

"True. That much?"

Natasha still kept quiet.

"Then, one evening, I got a call from a stranger who left an anonymous tip about the exact location of the money. That stranger was you. That was stage four."

Natasha smiled and said,

"You are now interested in stage three?"

"Yes"

Both laughed. Natasha said,

"I can trust you."

Ameya replied, "You are unnecessarily getting worried. When I knew you had called me to give the information, it was obvious that money was in your possession. You left the same at a designated place and called me from a landline number. And the fact that you called me is known only to me. It is known neither to my seniors nor to my juniors."

Natasha started speaking,

"I had a friend named Neelesh. We used to meet off and on. The money I had uncovered at my father's flat was a secret, I couldn't share it with anyone. I single-handedly decided and managed that it should be shipped abroad and chose Dubai as the destination. But when your department intercepted Mulliani's man, I got scared. I needed to confide in someone. I shared it with Neelesh then."

"Who is Neelesh?"

"He is a lawyer. But from the day I told him, he started behaving strangely. I could notice, but I could not figure out the reason. I kept meeting him."

Ameya kept listening. Natasha continued,

"His driver was earlier my driver. One fine day, his driver came to me requesting to find him another job. I asked him,

"Why, what happened?"

"Yesterday, the entire day, Neelesh sir was not at home. He had left before I came. I kept waiting. In the late evening, he came, and he saw me there. He called and told me to take two suitcases from the car and bring them upstairs to his flat. After that, he gave me some money and said, you need not come, as he was going abroad."

I asked the driver,

"What suitcases? Were they heavy?"

"Yes," he replied

"And what was the colour?"

"Light blue."

"Both."

"Yes, madam. Both of them."

"That was the first time I had serious doubts that Neelesh somehow got to the hideout and brought the suitcases. Those were light blue and were purchased by me."

"Your story is getting interesting," Ameya said.

Natasha continued, "I still wanted to be sure so I went to his house the following day. Then, on the pretext of using the washroom, I entered his bedroom. Well, there were two suitcases, the same colour and brand. We had lunch when he told me that he was leaving the next day for Singapore. I was dead sure that he was taking the money out of the country."

"That, too, would have solved your problem. The money was going out."

"Ameya, it was a huge amount. He was cheating on me. I couldn't tolerate it. I promised to come to his house the next day and drop him at the airport. Initially, he was reluctant, but then he agreed."

"But how did you get hold of the suitcases?" Ameya probed.

Natasha replied, "I am coming to that. I went to the same shop and bought two more suitcases, the same brand and colour. At night, I filled both with the old newspapers and magazines. Here, I had to take my driver into confidence. That part was a bit, risky but my driver is smart. Kuku kept the suitcases in the back of the car. I had told him that exactly the identical suitcases were to be picked up from Neelesh's house and that when you would unload those from the car at airport, you would take out *our* suitcases and not his suitcases. My job was to keep him distracted at the airport while dropping him off for a few minutes."

"That is easy for a woman."

"Yes, but not with a man, you have started despising. All went well as per plan. At the airport, Kuku brought the trolley, and kept the two suitcases while I embraced him in the car, and I had to give him a long kiss, which I hated. So, when we got down, his trolley was ready. He took it and went in."

"Pretty smart."

"Now, I was back to square one. What do I do with the money? I had two options. Either to carry the money to Dubai myself or to inform your department. I had your number."

"And you called me," Ameya said.

"It was not that simple. It was a huge amount of money," Natasha said. She took a pause and then said,

"In *Bhagwat Gita*, there is a chapter which says that there are three fundamental modes in each person's life – the mode of goodness; the mode of passion and the mode of ignorance. The fight for supremacy always goes on among these three modes. Allowing Neelesh to carry the money out, which he was set to do, was the mode of ignorance. I closed that mode there and then. When I was sitting in a hotel before entering the airport, I was in two minds. Mode of goodness compelled me to inform you and let the money go into proper hands. Mode of passion was to take the money out of India and get it disposed of somehow."

Ameya smiled and said,

"Mode of goodness prevailed."

"Yes."

"So, you found a workable solution for your problem."

"Workable but not lawful."

"You did a fine job. You could have allowed Neelesh to carry the money and given that information to me. We could have arrested him with the money."

Natasha remained silent and said slowly,

"I had thought that too, but I never wanted to get him arrested."

"You are in love with him."

"No."

"You were in love with him?"

"Never. It was just that we needed each other."

Ameya looked at Natasha. A woman in her late thirties had her needs. She asked,

"You both have not met after that?"

"No, on finding old newspapers in suitcases, he would know that I had done it. But then he was taking my money. He could never reveal that. And at my end, I would not try to meet someone whom I couldn't trust. He was the only person with whom I shared the recovery of three million dollars at my residence. He was taking advantage of that information."

There were tears in Natasha's eyes. Ameya got up and patted her shoulders. She said,

"Natasha, you are a strong woman."

"Thank you for your support."

Natasha got up. They shook hands. Ameya said,

"We are friends. You can come to my place any time, and we will have dinner together."

"Sure madam."

"Ameya," Ameya said.

Both laughed. Ameya left the restaurant. Natasha was looking relieved.

* * *

No one, however, knew that mode of passion had prevailed. Natasha had got the code from Sukhdev. On reaching Dubai that day, she got the money from Rashid after a deduction of fifty-five thousand US dollars. That was her secret and only hers.

* * * * *